THE SPIDER:
VOYAGE OF THE COFFIN SHIP

THE **MASTER** OF **MEN!**

VOYAGE OF
THE COFFIN SHIP

By Grant Stockbridge

STEEGER BOOKS • 2020

PUBLISHING HISTORY

"Voyage of the Coffin Ship" originally appeared in the June 1937 (Vol. 12, No. 1) issue
of *The Spider* magazine. Copyright 2020 by Argosy Communications, Inc. All rights
reserved.

CHAPTER 1
DANGER BOOKS PASSAGE

T HE LITTLE man lay in a crumpled heap behind two packing cases at the edge of the pier. A knife protruded from his back, and his coat was soggy with blood.

Richard Wentworth, sometimes known as the Spider, would never have discovered the little man, had it not been for the fact that he wanted to secure a vantage point on the pier, from which he could see all who went up the *Monrovia's* gangplank. Standing between those two packing cases, he was directly opposite the gangplank. He was watching tensely for Nita van Sloan, his fiancée, with whom he was to sail on a vacation. That is, it had begun as a vacation, but from the way things began to shape up, it might turn out to be a much more serious business. In the first place, Wentworth himself had to be careful not to be recognized here.

Officially, Richard Wentworth was dead. The enemies he had made, during the years when he fought the underworld relentlessly as the Spider, had finally caught an inkling of the truth—that the noted sportsman, the wealthy young society man whose pictures appeared in the rotogravures and who was known as Richard Wentworth, was also the night-shrouded figure whose two blazing automatics had cut down so many of their number.

Nita van Sloan had begged Wentworth often to give up the dangerous life of the Spider, and he had acquiesced. Not long

The rifle slug sent Sir John
crashing to the gangplank.

ago, the crushed body of a gangster had been found in the streets of New York, and Wentworth had seized the opportunity to pass that gangster off as himself.*

Officially dead, he had added a moustache, tufted eyebrows, sideburns and a few other cunning touches of makeup to his appearance, and had converted himself into one Pierre Colain, wealthy landowner of Senegal. With the aid of a passport and other papers acquired through friends in Washington, he had arranged to sail today on the *Queen Mary,* which was berthed at a dock several miles from this one. But a note from Nita van Sloan, received at the last moment, had changed those plans, had brought him here. That note lay in his pocket now. It read:

Dick Darling:

We must change our plans. Please do exactly as I say. I'll explain later. We are sailing on the *Monrovia* instead of the *Queen Mary.* I've bought tickets for both of us. You have stateroom number 16, on A Deck, and I have number 18. You remember Sir John Swinnerton? He'll have number 20. It's for him we're changing our plans—for him and his niece, Georgia.

Dick, Sir John is in mortal danger. I'll arrive at the *Monrovia's* pier at exactly four-twenty, with Sir John and his niece. Be there. Watch us, follow us onto the ship. *But on no account must you speak to us.* I'll explain after we sail; and forgive me for asking so much of you, Dick.

* Author's Note: Readers are referred to the novel appearing in the preceding adventure, entitled "The Devil's Pawnbroker," for details of the incident referred to above.

Nita.

Wentworth knew why Sir John Swinnerton was sailing on the *Monrovia*. His glance went to the four armored cars at the far end of the pier, where stevedores were unloading forty-four boxes of bullion destined for the Bank of England. Sir John was the financial advisor to the Bank of England, and he was accompanying this shipment from the Federal Reserve Bank.

Police and Treasury guards were surrounding the trucks in a solid semicircle. It was apparent that any attempt against that gold here on the pier would be foredoomed to failure.

Wentworth's glance traveled down to the other end of the pier, where a cargo even more strange was being loaded into hatch number one by the forward winch. That cargo consisted of twenty-four coffins!

They contained the bodies of Japanese, who were being shipped home for burial. Wentworth recalled reading in the paper of the bus accident in Michigan where twenty-four Japanese students had been thrown from a bridge in the bus, and drowned. Wentworth had a smattering of Japanese, and his eyes narrowed as be noted that though the coffins were hermetically sealed in accordance with sea regulation, there were little dots appearing after some of the Japanese characters, which had no place there. He was hardly a master of Nippon's language, but he knew there was something wrong with those characters.

He shrugged. There would be time enough to examine them when he got on board. There could be little besides corpses in those coffins.

And suddenly, he stiffened. He was conscious of being

stared at. The man who was looking at him was a little Japanese, immaculately dressed, who stood near the coffins. Immediately recognition flashed upon Wentworth. That man was Baron Kawashi Otuna!

MEMORIES FIFTEEN years old suddenly flooded Wentworth with teeming recollections. That dapper little aristocratic Japanese who was watching the loading of the coffins had not changed a bit in fifteen years.

Thin, ascetic-looking, carefully dressed in cutaway and spats, with a gold-knobbed cane and gold-rimmed eyeglasses, Baron Kawashi Otuna resembled more a studious scholar or scientist than the rapacious, unscrupulous arms smuggler that he really was.

But Wentworth knew that there would probably be a small but effective pistol hidden somewhere about Otuna's dapper person; and he also knew that the gold-knobbed stick was in reality a sword-cane, which the Baron could use with all the skill of an expert fencer—and with as much deadliness.

Baron Kawashi Otuna was an immensely wealthy man, who always reached for more. He was as daring an adventurer as Wentworth himself—but more dangerous because his motives were selfish. Human life, which was cheap enough in the Far East, meant nothing to Otuna when weighed in the balance with possible further gain to himself.

Wentworth's last encounter with Otuna had been fifteen years before, in Outer Mongolia. He had disrupted a caravan under the Baron's leadership—a caravan bringing precious merchandise out of the West. That merchandise had consisted

of beautiful young girls who were to
be sold for profit. Kawashi Otuna
had himself escaped. But Wentworth
knew that the man hated him with all
the fierceness of which only Otuna
was capable.

Wentworth did not want to be
recognized today—above all, not by
Kawashi Otuna. The little man had turned away quickly, but
Wentworth wondered if his disguise was good enough to defy
the piercing inspection of this man.

He stepped a little further back between the two cases, and it
was then that he discovered the protruding foot of the little man.

His eyes narrowed, and he stepped behind the case, bent to
feel the man's heart. He was dead, but he had not been dead
more than twenty minutes. His pockets were turned inside out.
His face was frozen in the expression of terrible surprise that
must have assailed him when the knife was thrust into his back.

Wentworth's blood ran hotter at the thought of the cold-
blooded murder that had been committed here. For a moment
he considered showing the body to the police. Then he reflected
that he could do the dead man no good, and only involve himself
in needless questioning and investigation which might pierce
his disguise. The man would be found soon enough, anyway.

Wentworth steeled himself to leave the poor chap there.
He stood up, made sure there was no blood on his clothes, and
moved back to his point of vantage. It hurt him to do this, but
he had to remember that he was *Monsieur* Pierre Colain of

Senegal, and no longer Richard Wentworth, *alias* the Spider. And he intended to admonish Nita van Sloan when he saw her on the boat. He was going on a vacation now, and he wanted no part of adventure.

The dead man behind the packing case bothered him. Nita had said in the note that Sir John Swinnerton would be in danger. Whether that danger was linked in any way to this poor chap, he could not tell. Nor could he tell whether Baron Kawashi Otuna and his twenty-four coffins were connected with it in any way.

Abruptly, he thrust those thoughts behind him. He had caught sight of Nita van Sloan. She was hurrying down the pier toward the gangplank, accompanied by two persons whom he recognized. One was the elderly Sir John Swinnerton, whom he would have known at a glance; the other must be his adopted niece, Georgia.

WENTWORTH DREW in his breath at the startling beauty of this girl, whom he remembered only as a toddling child, many years back. Georgia Swinnerton and Nita van Sloan were walking on either side of Sir John, and all three seemed apprehensive of some sort of attack.

Unconsciously, Wentworth compared the beauty of the two women. Nita van Sloan's was more of the regal type. She walked with her back straight and her chin up, her expensively tailored dress setting off to glorious advantage the firm contours of her svelte figure. His eyes glowed for a moment as they followed her, forgetful now of Baron Kawashi Otuna, and of the twenty-four coffins. He had always loved Nita, and he always would.

Between these two there was an almost telepathic under-standing, which had often aroused their wonder. Even now, that curious telepathy was manifest. Although Nita had not seen Wentworth's disguise, although she could not be expected to recognize him in this crowd, she seemed to be sure that he was watching her; and as if guided by an unerring instinct, her eyes traveled over the throng, settled upon his tall figure. She smiled fleetingly for an instant, and then at once her glance flicked away from him. She had said in her note that he was not to speak to her. Then she must expect that she and her party would be watched—perhaps attacked, if their attitude was any criterion.

Carefully, Wentworth scanned the faces of the crowd, in an effort to ascertain if anyone was taking particular interest in them. He could find no sign that they were followed, or even watched. Turning casually for a second, he noted that even Baron Kawashi Otuna was at the far end of the dock, once more watching the last coffin as it was loaded into the cargo net to be hoisted up by the winch.

Nita and her two companions reached the gangplank. They stopped for a moment at the desk of the ship's purser, to have their tickets checked, and then they started up the narrow plank.

And it was at that instant that Wentworth spotted the danger.

No man of ordinary powers of observation would have noted it; or if he had, would have recognized it for what it was, or attached any particular significance to it.

But Wentworth saw it, knew it for what it was, understood the threat of it.

Far up on A Deck, where the passengers had not yet spread,

NITA VAN SLOAN

almost directly under the bridge, where he would be in shadow, stood a man. He seemed to be leaning against the rail in such fashion that only the top of his head and part of his face was visible. And alongside that white patch of face was a squat, small object that seemed to be attached to a rod of some kind.

Wentworth's first glance told him what that object was. It

was the muzzle of a short-barreled rifle, to which a silencer was screwed. And the man up there on A Deck was aiming directly down at Nita and her two friends!

Which of the three was his target, it was impossible to tell. And Wentworth did not wait to find out. The distance was not too great for an automatic, but the angle was deceptive and difficult. Nevertheless, Wentworth went into action. In the past he had been compelled to shoot at more elusive objects, with life in the balance, and he did not hesitate now.

His right hand snaked up and out from his shoulder holster. And in almost the same continuous motion his thumb flicked off the safety and he fired.

Simultaneously with his shot, a thin tongue of flame spurted from the muzzle of the rifle up on A Deck. The sniper up there had fired at the same instant. Wentworth had been a split-second too late!

But no!

His slug grazed the railing, smashed into the face of the killer up there. And the slug from the rifle, instead of striking Sir John Swinnerton in the heart, where it had no doubt been aimed, hit him in the shoulder, whirled him around and sent him crashing to the gangplank.

Georgia Swinnerton screamed, and Nita van Sloan sprang to the assistance of the wounded financial expert.

At once the dock became a scene of bedlam and excitement. Women shrieked, and men milled wildly against one another, not knowing what had happened, thinking perhaps that some attempt was being made against the gold bullion boxes, of which they all knew.

No one seemed to have seen the rifleman on A Deck, or the tall foreign-looking man on the dock who had drawn and fired with such lightning swiftness as to defy the human eye.

The police closed in on the spot where Sir John lay, and Nita van Sloan pointed up toward A Deck, telling them where the shot had come from. In the meantime, *Monsieur* Pierre Colain faded back into the crowd, having replaced the automatic in its holster.

HE HAD no desire to make known the fact that he had been involved in the incident; for though his passport and papers were in perfect order, questions might be embarrassing, and might prevent his sailing on the *Monrovia*. And from the way things were beginning to shape up, Wentworth wanted more than anything else to make that trip with the boxes of bullion and the twenty-four coffins—and Baron Kawashi Otuna.

Thought of Baron Otuna caused him to glance down toward the foot of the pier. He could not see whether the Jap was there, due to the press of the crowd. But he saw that the last of the coffins was being lowered into the forward hatch, just as if nothing had happened.

Wentworth turned back toward the scene at the gangplank. The ship's doctor was running down toward where Sir John lay, and Nita van Sloan was holding a tiny bit of lace handkerchief to the wounded man's shoulder.

The police, in response to Nita's information, were swarming up onto the ship in search of the mysterious rifleman. Went-

worth's lips pursed into a thin line. When they found that rifleman's body, with a thirty-eight caliber slug in his head, they would begin searching for a man with an automatic. They would be able to tell, of course, that the shot had come from the dock, by the fact that the railing was nicked, as well as by the angle of the shot. Wentworth didn't want to be on the dock when they began looking; so he moved over toward the purser's table.

The police had established order on the dock once more, and he could hear Sir John talking to the captain in charge of the police, while the ship's doctor attended to his wound.

"The doctor tells me," Sir John was saying, "that he will have little difficulty in probing for the bullet, and that it is merely a flesh wound. Therefore it will be unnecessary for me to remain here. It is imperative that I sail with the gold."

"I'm sorry, sir," the police captain replied, "but you'll have to stay. We'll find the man who fired that shot, all right, and you'll have to press charges."

Wentworth, listening to the conversation from where he stood at the purser's table, smiled tightly. They would find the man who fired the shot all right—with a slug in his head!

The purser was looking up at him, frowning. "What is it, sir?"

"You have a ticket, here," Wentworth asked him, "in the name of Pierre Colain? I am *Monsieur* Colain, if you please."

The purser riffled his papers, and after scanning Wentworth's proofs of identity, passed over the ticket. Wentworth started for the gangplank. He had missed part of the altercation between Sir John and the police captain, but now he caught the tail end of it.

"—and I tell you," Sir John was insisting, "that if you will phone Washington they'll cut all this red tape! I have a diplomatic passport, officer, and you have no right to detain me!"

The police captain shrugged. "All right, sir, if you insist. Get a stretcher, doc, and take him on board."

Wentworth sighed in relief. He had been afraid for a moment that Nita would have to remain behind with Sir John, as a witness. Now that he knew she was coming, he hurried up the gangplank. Passengers were crowding the rail, asking questions of everyone who came aboard. No one knew exactly what had happened, except that the police were searching the ship.

Wentworth frowned, perplexed. Nita had told the police where the shot had come from, and the searchers should have had no difficulty in finding the body of the marksman up there. Wentworth knew with absolute certainty that he had killed the man; and the fellow could not have walked or crawled away from the rail with his head blown off.

Two of the ship's stewards were carrying Sir John Swinnerton up the gangplank on a stretcher, and Nita and Georgia Swinnerton were following.

Wentworth, satisfied that they were aboard the ship, moved out of the crowd, over to the elevator. He went up to A Deck, and looked around. Several uniformed police were standing in a small semicircle near the rail where the rifleman had lurked. They were examining something on the deck.

Of the man whom Wentworth had killed, there was no sign! Wentworth joined the police, just as a portly man in the uniform of a sea captain came down from the bridge. This was Captain Homan, master of the *Monrovia*. The police were manifestly puzzled. One of them said to Captain Homan:

"We thought that young woman was mistaken when she said the shot came from here, sir. But she must have been right. Look at the blood right here. And look at that mess by the rail. Someone must have shot this rifleman, too—blown his brains out, if you ask me. But there's no sign of the guy!"

Captain Homan looked incredulous. "Don't tell me," he boomed, "that the man had his brains shot out, and then went away from here!"

"No, sir," the policeman replied. "But someone might have carried him away."

Captain Homan scoffed. "Impossible! It's true there was no one here on A Deck at the time. But there are a couple of barmen in the bar right back there, and there must have been half a dozen stewards in the salon. They would have seen anyone carrying a dead man—and you can be sure they would have stopped him!"

The policeman shrugged. "But there's the blood. You can see for yourself."

"All right," Captain Homan barked. "Search the ship. But make it fast. We're ten minutes late already, and orders from the Treasury Department are to let nothing keep that bullion from leaving on time!"

CHAPTER 2
PIRATES TO STARBOARD

THE *Monrovia* sailed an hour and a half late. The police, aided by reserves from the precinct house, had found nothing at all on board. Not a single trace of the missing rifleman had been turned up.

Wentworth engaged one of the ship's officers in conversation, and learned that a United States destroyer was steaming up from Newport News to act as a convoy. A British cruiser would meet them a day or two out, also. But when the destroyer was to pick them up, the officer either did not know, or would not tell.

All the passengers knew of the incident on the dock, as well as of the mysterious rifleman. And as a result there was a good deal of nervous tension aboard the liner. The presence of that huge fortune in gold made everybody a bit jittery.

In addition, the presence of the twenty-four coffins in the forward hatch did nothing to soothe the prevailing nervousness. The crew were obviously uneasy. The stewards were jumpy, careless in their service. The passengers, worried and ill at ease, talked nervously in small groups, and fear showed in the eyes of many.

Wentworth spent most of the afternoon prowling about the ship. He knew very well that there must be someone aboard who had been in league with the murderous rifleman, who had carried the dead body away from the rail and hidden it. Somewhere on the *Monrovia* was a hiding place that had been overlooked by the searchers. Somewhere, in cabin, in a hold or crew quarters, hidden from the watchful eyes of officers and men, were those who plotted to gain possession of the twenty million in gold.

If a destroyer was scheduled to meet the *Monrovia*, then the plotters would have to work fast. They would have to strike tonight.

What they had hoped to gain by killing Sir John Swinnerton, he could not understand. Nita might know, but he had been unable to talk to her. All afternoon she had remained in Cabin 20, with Georgia Swinnerton and her wounded uncle. Wentworth returned to his cabin at frequent intervals in the hope that Nita might have left a note for him. But there was nothing.

Upon returning to his stateroom to change for dinner, he did finally find a note. But it was not from Nita. He frowned as he read it. It was upon the embossed stationery of the *Monrovia*, and it read as follows:

> Captain Homan requests the pleasure of your presence at his table at dinner tonight.

The note was addressed to *Monsieur* Pierre Colain, which was strange, in view of the fact that Captain Homan had probably never heard of Pierre Colain before. It is generally regarded as a signal honor among the passengers to be invited to sit at the captain's table. Only persons of note receive such an invitation.

Wentworth was worried by it. But he dressed carefully, wiping and cleaning the automatic which he had used that afternoon, before putting it away in his baggage. It was just possible that his room might be searched while he was at dinner. He put a fresh clip into the automatic, and on his way to the dining room he dropped the old clip over the side. For the occasion he provided himself with a small, twenty-two caliber pistol, which sat snugly in an inner pocket of his tuxedo, where it would not make too much of a bulge.

WHEN HE appeared in the dining room, most of the other passengers were already seated. His distinguished appearance attracted the gaze of many of the women in the room, and their eyes followed him admiringly as he was led to the captain's table at the far end of the dining room.

He stiffened almost imperceptibly as he noted that Nita van Sloan, Georgia Swinnerton and Baron Kawashi Otuna were among the six persons seated with the captain. Captain Homan nodded genially and rose as Wentworth came to a halt beside him, returning his bow.

"Monsieur Pierre Colain, it will be a great pleasure to have you at this table during the voyage. I have heard a great deal about you!"

Wentworth raised his eyebrows. Had Nita deliberately mentioned his name to Homan so as to bring him here? A single glance at Nita's puzzled expression told him that this was not so. She was as much mystified by the unexplained honor as was he.

"I am sure," he replied to Homan, "that the pleasure will be entirely mine!"

He found that his chair was between that of a dark-haired vivacious widow, Mrs. Burgeon, on his right, and Baron Kawashi Otuna on his left.

Captain Homan, who sat one chair away, at Mrs. Burgeon's right, went on: "And now, *Monsieur* Colain, you must know my other guests." He motioned to Nita, who sat at his right, across the table from Wentworth. "Miss Nita van Sloan, of New York. The gentleman next to her is Mr. Oscar Potts, of San Francisco. The young lady next to Mr. Potts is Miss Georgia Swinnerton, niece of Sir John,  who—er—met with an unfortunate accident this afternoon. We trust that he will soon be well enough to join us."

Nita had merely nodded her head in acknowledgment of the introduction. Oscar Potts, apparently a wealthy businessman, was plainly out of his element here. He was a bit flustered at the honor of sitting at the captain's table. Wentworth noted that he wore the blue jacket and white flannels of a yachting commodore.

Potts said embarrassedly: "I—I—my wife is ill, too, you know. I hated to leave her alone, but when the captain invited me, she sort of insisted that I accept. It isn't every day you're invited to dine with the captain of a transatlantic liner!"

"I see you are a seafaring man, too, Commodore Potts," Wentworth said with a twinkle in his eye.

"Oh, yes, *Monsieur* Colain. Back in Frisco I got lost one time—"

"Yes, yes," Captain Homan interrupted, laughing. "You've already told us about the time you were lost off the coast of California. Now just let me finish the introductions. I'm sure *Monsieur* Colain will want to meet all of us."

"Sure, sure," Potts said uncertainly, subsiding into his chair.

Captain Homan went on: "The very stern-looking chap next to Miss Swinnerton is my First Officer, Captain Stanton Macy. He holds a master's license himself, so if anything should ever happen to me, you needn't worry—he'll get you across. And on your left, *Monsieur* Colain, is Baron Kawashi Otuna of Japan."

Kawashi Otuna was smiling slyly as he acknowledged the introduction. His small eyes peered out from the horn-rimmed glasses, with a glint that was almost malicious.

Wentworth said with an affectation of casualness: "I have heard of Baron Otuna as an international personage."

Kawashi Otuna smiled thinly. "Thank you, *Monsieur* Colain. And if I remember correctly, *Monsieur*, I was privileged to meet you some years ago in Mongolia—"

"How interesting!" exclaimed Mrs. Burgeon, who sat at Wentworth's right, between himself and Captain Macy. "Mongolia must be a fascinating country. They say the people drink nothing but goat's milk. Tell us about Mongolia, *Monsieur* Colain!"

Mrs. Burgeon was dressed in a daringly low-cut evening gown, and her face was flushed and pretty. In spite of that, there was a calculating sort of gleam in her eyes that Wentworth did not like. He said coldly: "Unfortunately, *Madame,* I will have to leave such description to *Monsieur le Baron.*"

THEY HAD ordered their cocktails, and now the first course of the dinner was being served. Wentworth saw that Nita was eating nervously, throwing an occasional quick glance at him as if she wished to warn him of some imminent danger. Georgia Swinnerton toyed with her food. Mr. Potts, at her left, made several flippant remarks, to which she paid but scant attention.

She cast several apprehensive glances at First Officer Stanton Macy, on her right.

The captain had already mentioned that due to the presence of the bullion on board, the first officer and the captain were standing their trick on the bridge together, and would therefore eat at the same table.

Macy was a big, raw-boned, weather-beaten man, with an almost surly look in his eyes. The only ones who seemed to be really enjoying the dinner were Baron Kawashi Otuna and Mrs. Burgeon, and their gaiety was more or less strained. In fact, a tight air of tension appeared to pervade the entire dining salon.

Captain Homan's guests fell silent, and in the lull, Mrs. Burgeon returned again to the subject of Mongolia.

"You must have had some exciting adventures in Mongolia, dear Baron Otuna," she said bubblingly. "Do tell us some of them!"

Otuna smiled slyly. "My poor adventures are really nothing, Mrs. Burgeon. But there was one man who could tell you stories by the hour about Mongolia, if he were here." Otuna sighed in mock regret. "Alas, but he is dead." He looked up suddenly, staring squarely at Wentworth. "I refer to a man named Richard Wentworth. You knew him, perhaps?"

Nita started perceptibly, as did Georgia Swinnerton. Suddenly, everybody at the table seemed to have become taut, waiting for *Monsieur* Colain's answer.

"I have heard of him," Wentworth replied placidly. "He was an interesting man. Unfortunate that he was killed."

"Unfortunate?" Otuna caught him up. "Would you say it was

unfortunate that the man who was really the Spider should have been killed? Would you say it was unfortunate that the greatest criminal of the age should have met his just deserts—"

He was interrupted by a low exclamation from Nita van Sloan, who pushed her chair back from the table, started to rise.

"You will excuse me," she said in a low voice.

Georgia Swinnerton's eyes were blazing. "You cad!" she flung at Otuna. "Don't you know that Miss van Sloan is wearing mourning for Richard Wentworth? Don't you know that she was his fiancée?"

Baron Otuna arose quickly, his face a mask of contrite apology. "I had no idea, Miss van Sloan, I assure you. I beg of you, do not leave us."

Nita permitted herself to be induced to remain, mainly at Georgia Swinnerton's insistence.

Otuna apologized humbly, though Wentworth felt he detected a note of mockery under that humbleness. Otuna was not through yet. He had had a definite object in dragging the Spider's name into the conversation.

Wentworth felt only admiration for Nita. Her acting had been perfect. She had expressed just the proper amount of indignation that might be expected of a bereaved fiancée. But he could see that she was still apprehensive of something yet to come.

Now the conversation turned to the events of the afternoon, and everyone began to speculate as to who could have shot Sir John Swinnerton, and as to what had happened to the rifleman.

As a matter of fact, that had been the major topic of conversation at all the other tables in the dining salon.

Mrs. Burgeon seemed to think it was all very exciting and romantic, having twenty million dollars in gold on board. "And wouldn't it be thrilling," she exclaimed, "if a ship full of pirates were to attack us!"

"Lady," said Mr. Oscar Potts, "you wouldn't think it was thrilling if those pirates were to hang us all when they got through pillaging the ship!"

Captain Homan laughed. "You people talk about pirates as if we were living a hundred years ago. We have no pirates these days—"

"Except in China," Kawashi Otuna broke in. The Jap turned to Wentworth. "Have you ever been in China, *Monsieur* Colain? As a matter of fact, you haven't told us yet whether you were ever in Mongolia."

Captain Homan spoke before Wentworth could answer. "I thought you told me you knew *Monsieur* Colain many years ago, Baron Otuna. In fact, that was my understanding when you suggested that I invite him to join us."

Wentworth tautened. Then it was Otuna who was responsible for his being here. The Jap had planned this cross-examination.

Kawashi replied smoothly: "Indeed, I am sure that I have met *Monsieur* Colain before today. But—*he went under another name then!*"

Abruptly there was a hush at the table.

FIRST OFFICER Stanton Macy threw a quick side glance at Georgia Swinnerton. Nita van Sloan sat tensely, watching

Wentworth. Oscar Potts stared from one to the other, uncomprehendingly. Even Mrs. Burgeon was silent. Nobody touched the food. They all sensed that something momentous was about to take place.

Kawashi Otuna went on smoothly, his small gimlet eyes fixed unblinkingly on Wentworth.

"You were not known as Pierre Colain when I encountered you in Mongolia. Shall I tell these people who you really are? Or would you prefer to tell them yourself?"

Wentworth met his gaze calmly. "I think, my dear Baron, that the events of this afternoon must have affected you queerly. Perhaps you had better go to your cabin and lie down. A little sedative, perhaps—"

Otuna broke in sharply. "You can't talk your way out of this,

A shell from the yacht's six-inch gun
had struck squarely amidships!

my friend. Since you won't tell them, I will!" He raised his voice, and the diners at the nearby tables turned to listen.

"You are Richard Wentworth, alias the Spider! I was sure of it when I saw your eyes. Now I am doubly sure!" He pointed dramatically at Nita. "There is your fiancée. You led the world to believe that you were dead, and you sailed under another name. But Miss van Sloan is still with you. You are the Spider—the greatest criminal of the age! And you're on board this ship for the purpose of stealing the gold ingots in the hold. Deny it if you can!"

Captain Homan said gravely: "That is a serious charge, Baron Otuna. Have you any proof? After all, *Monsieur* Colain's papers are all in order—"

"Yes, I have proof!" Kawashi cut in savagely. "Search this man's cabin. You will find there the gun with which Sir John Swinnerton was shot. It was this man who shot him!"

"That's not true!" Nita van Sloan interrupted. *"Monsieur* Colain was behind us on the dock, and Sir John was shot from the ship—from in front." She turned to Georgia Swinnerton. "You saw that, didn't you, Georgia?"

Otuna laughed sourly. "You see? This proves my statement. Miss van Sloan is known to have been Richard Wentworth's fiancée. He left her all his property. And now she hastens to protect *Monsieur* Colain, whom she pretends never to have met before tonight—yet she knows where he stood on the dock, this afternoon!"

Wentworth rose abruptly. "All this proves nothing. Baron Otuna has charged that the gun which wounded Sir John Swinnerton will be found in my stateroom. Let my cabin be searched. I have no objection."

He took the key from his pocket, dropped it on the table.

"Fair enough," said Captain Homan. He raised his voice. "Mr. Macy! Get the Master-at-Arms. Have him accompany you while you search *Monsieur* Colain's cabin. Take one of the junior officers with you, as an additional witness to what you find."

Stanton Macy saluted. Wentworth took a key ring from his pocket, slipped off three small keys. "These will open my steamer trunk and bags," he told the first officer.

He refrained from informing Macy that in each of his bags, as well as in the steamer trunk, was a cleverly concealed false bottom, which would defy detection by expert searchers. It was here that he had placed his automatics and various other sundry items that he did not wish to be exposed to prying eyes. Among those sundry items were a certain black cape and a slouch hat which were the identifying attire of the Spider. Also hidden in those bags was the seal of the Spider, which had appeared upon the forehead of many a dead gangster to whom the blazing automatics of the Spider had brought swift retributive justice.

There were ingenious instruments in those hidden compartments, and makeup material by means of which Wentworth could alter his appearance radically in time of emergency. Any of those items, if discovered, would immediately brand Richard Wentworth as the greatest criminal of the age. For, due to the unconventional methods used by the Spider in fighting crime, the law had branded him a criminal, put a price upon his head. Even now that he was supposed to be dead, however, no one could definitely prove that Richard Wentworth had been the Spider.

That was the devilish part of Baron Kawashi Otuna's plan. The Jap must have shrewdly deduced that Wentworth would not travel without the paraphernalia of the Spider. He no doubt expected that a thorough search of Wentworth's baggage would reveal some such paraphernalia; and once Pierre Colain stood exposed as the Spider, all suspicion in connection with the shooting of Sir John Swinnerton and the disappearance of the rifleman would at once turn to Colain.

MACY TOOK the keys and left the dining room, followed by the curious gaze of all the passengers. Many of them had forgotten their meals, but they were staying to see the denouement of the strange drama being played out at the captain's table. They had not heard the details of the conversation, but they could gather that something was occurring in connection with the mysterious shooting of the afternoon. And many of the women in the room felt sympathy for the tall, handsome French gentleman who was apparently under suspicion.

Captain Homan looked around the table, then growled to Wentworth: "You may as well seat yourself again, *Monsieur* Colain, till Mr. Macy returns. I don't mind saying that if it's proved that you are Richard Wentworth, I shall have to notify the New York police, and hold you on board for the return trip."

Wentworth smiled as he sat down. "In the event that this charge against me is not proved, Captain Homan, I suggest that you radio the destroyer which is to meet you, to hurry. I must warn you that I fear some sort of attempt will soon be made to seize the boxes of bullion in your hold."

Homan shrugged. "The destroyer meets us in the morning. What could anyone do overnight? Even if they seized the ship, where could they take it? Of course, it's ridiculous even to think of such a thing. Every member of the crew is reliable. The passengers are all *bona fide*, known by their passports. The ship was searched thoroughly, so it's certain that there are no stowaways—"

"What of the twenty-four coffins that Baron Kawashi Otuna here has charge of? Suppose they contained live gunmen instead of dead Japanese—"

Kawashi laughed coldly. "Very clever, my friend—but not good enough. Captain Homan was down in the hold with me this afternoon, and inspected those coffins. They are all hermetically sealed. If there were a live man in any of them, he would suffocate."

"That is true," Captain Homan said. "And don't think you can turn attention from yourself by bringing up those coffins. They're all shipshape, and as the Baron says, a man couldn't live in them. I—"

He was interrupted by the sudden entrance of one of the junior officers, who made his way hurriedly across the room toward the table.

Homan frowned, watching his approach. "I wonder what's the matter," Wentworth heard him mutter. "That's Vinson. It's his trick on the bridge!"

Mrs. Burgeon said inanely: "Maybe the ship is sinking. That would certainly be exciting—"

She subsided at a dark look from Homan, and threw Wentworth a glance that was expressive of resignation. "Believe me, *Monsieur* Colain, I think you innocent, no matter what anyone says."

Wentworth thanked her with a smile, and turned away from her just as the junior officer stepped up to the table.

Captain Homan rumbled: "What is it, Vinson?"

The junior officer hesitated, looked at the others around the table. "If you'll excuse me, sir, I think you'd better come up to the bridge."

Just then they became conscious that the steady throb of the propellers had ceased. The ship was slowing down!

Homan barked: "You might as well tell me what it is right here, Vinson. These people will think the worst anyway. What's the reason we're losing way?"

Vinson was extraordinarily pale. "Sir, it's almost unbelievable. But there's a yacht to leeward, a hundred and twenty footer, flying the skull and crossbones, and she mounts a six-inch gun in her bows!"

Homan's mouth dropped open. "What?"

Vinson had spoken very low, so that only those at the captain's table could hear. Now he nodded.

"It's true, sir!" He jerked his head toward the dining salon portholes, on the starboard side. "Look for yourself, Captain. You can see her from here. I don't want to point, for fear of creating a panic among the other passengers."

VOYAGE OF THE COFFIN SHIP

HOMAN THREW a quick glance to his right. Wentworth followed his gaze, and his eyes narrowed at what he saw. The night was fairly clear, and visibility was good for a great distance.

Clearly visible were the riding lights of a ship, and the craft's outline could be seen easily because of two powerful searchlights. Those lights were turned downward, so that it was possible to distinguish the trim lines of a modern, up-to-date yacht. And the rays of the yacht's after-searchlight shone upon a black flag at the masthead—a flag upon which were painted the gruesome insignia of piratical craft in the shape of a skull and crossbones. The bow searchlight illuminated a long gun mounted forward of the yacht's bridge.

Homan's mouth was still open. He clamped it shut with a snap. "This is impossible! Piracy on the high seas! But why are you slowing us up, Vinson? Why have you ordered the engines stopped?"

"Because, sir, we've been in communication with her. She signaled us by blinkers. Here is the message she sent!"

Vinson handed the captain a scribbled sheet of paper. Homan read it, and all the color left his face. "By God!" he exclaimed. "I can't believe it!"

His hand dropped to the table, and Wentworth could read the message that had been taken down from the heliograph signals:

S.S. *Monrovia:*

This is the Motor Yacht *Sea Master,* under command of "The Baron." Heave to at once and await our boarding party, or take the consequences. We mount a six-inch gun, and we'll sink you if you disobey!

Mrs. Burgeon, at the captain's left, and Nita and Mr. Potts on the other side had all read the message with Wentworth. Oscar Potts groaned.

"My God, this is terrible! My wife! She's got a bad heart, and must be kept from excitement. A thing like this may kill her!"

Homan's lips tightened. "I'll be damned if I'll knuckle under to a threat like that! They wouldn't dare to sink us. The whole United States Navy would be after them in an hour. Vinson, order full steam ahead! We've got the legs of that yacht, and we'll pull away from her. And radio an appeal for help. The destroyer *Marchand* is steaming to meet us. Tell them to snap it up, for God's sake!"

Vinson hesitated. "They sound like they mean business, sir. And they're within range. A well-placed shot beneath our water line—"

"Do as I say, Vinson!" Captain Homan ordered. "Since when have you undertaken to question my orders?"

"Y-yes, sir," Vinson stammered. He saluted and, walking jerkily, disappeared through the forward dining salon entrance, heading for the bridge.

Homan stood up, facing the sea of staring faces in the salon. "Ladies and gentlemen," he announced in a firm voice, "there is no cause for alarm. Sea pirates ceased to exist a hundred years ago. Please continue with your meal."

He seated himself, glared around the table. "I should have known it," he muttered. "Corpses were never lucky for a ship. It's those damned corpses of yours, Baron Otuna."

The Jap shrugged. "Personally, Captain, I think it's the gold. And if you were to dig into this a little more deeply, you'd probably find that our good friend, *Monsieur* Colain, is in league with that yacht—"

He paused as First Officer Stanton Macy, followed by the Master-at-Arms, entered the dining room. They were trailed by a junior officer, who remained at the door, on guard, as if to prevent anyone leaving.

Wentworth's eyes narrowed, and he felt a cold tingle down the back of his spine as he saw what Macy carried. The first officer was holding a Lee-Enfield rifle, to the muzzle of which a silencer had been attached.

Macy stepped up to the table, and nodded to the Master-at-Arms, who significantly moved over and stood behind Wentworth's chair. Then the First Officer held up the rifle.

"This," he said slowly, "is what I found hidden in *Monsieur* Colain's room!"

CHAPTER 3
THE SEA MASTER'S WARNING

THE ACCUSTOMED throbbing of the engines had begun again. But no one seemed to notice it, except Wentworth. The others were all staring in shocked silence at the Lee-Enfield in Macy's big hands.

The implication was clear. No speech was necessary. But Macy added: "It was hung by a string, over the side of his deck terrace. I found it only by accident."

Oscar Potts exclaimed: "Oh, Lord! That must be the rifle that Sir John was shot with!"

Macy nodded grimly. "It checks so far, though we haven't the facilities for comparing the bullets. Sir John was shot with a bullet of this caliber."

Baron Kawashi Otuna threw a malicious, triumphant glance at Wentworth. "It was clever, *Monsieur* Colain, to hang the rifle over the side of the ship."

Wentworth's glance traveled from face to face around the table. Nita van Sloan's eyes were wide with apprehension. Georgia Swinnerton was gazing at the Lee-Enfield uncomprehendingly. Oscar Potts was shaking his head lugubriously. Even Mrs. Burgeon, who had expressed such confidence in him a moment ago, was looking doubtful.

And over the entire dining room there had fallen a strange hush. The people at the other tables, not as yet fully cognizant of the menace of the pirate yacht, were staring with growing uneasiness at the captain's table. Wentworth, aware of his own danger, was far more concerned with the graver peril which each passing moment brought closer to the entire ship's company.

He arose slowly, while the Master-at-Arms stood tensely behind him. "Of course, Captain," he said to Homan, "you must admit the possibility that this rifle was placed in my cabin by someone other than myself?"

Homan's eyes were unsympathetic. "There is that possibility, *Monsieur* Colain. But we are facing an emergency. We are apparently to be attacked by a pirate ship, whose purpose is to seize the gold we are carrying. In view of Baron Otuna's accusation, I can see only one course of action at this time, in the interests of our passengers. I must place you in custody. If you are innocent, you will be given ample opportunity to prove it."

"Perhaps not," Wentworth said bitterly. "While you are wasting your suspicions on me, the *Monrovia* may be sunk—sent to the bottom of the sea!"

"I don't think so," Homan replied gravely. "This note from the yacht is just a bluff. They wouldn't dare to fire at us. By this time the *Marchand* must have been notified, and is steaming toward us at full speed. Other United States vessels will be converging on us. That yacht could never hope to escape—"

Nita van Sloan broke in desperately: "That note, Captain. It's signed 'The Baron,' isn't it?"

"What of it, miss?"

Nita threw an expressive glance at Kawashi Otuna. "We have a Baron here among us."

Homan laughed harshly. "Are you suggesting that Baron Kawashi would give himself away like that if he were really in league with the yacht? No, Miss van Sloan, I'm afraid your efforts to divert attention from *Monsieur* Colain are futile."

He swung to face Wentworth. "*Monsieur* Colain, I regret that I am compelled to place you in custody." He raised his voice. "Master-at-Arms! Place *Monsieur* Pierre Colain under arrest, and turn him over to the Master of the Brig. He is to be held there, incommunicado, until further orders!"

The Master-at-Arms saluted, and placed a hand on Wentworth's shoulder. First Officer Macy put down the rifle and,

The green men engulfed Captain Homan. Knives gleamed.

drawing a revolver, stepped around the table and took up a position at Wentworth's left.

"Just in case anybody tries a rescue!" he said significantly.

WENTWORTH SHRUGGED. The ship was moving faster now, her twin screws revolving at full speed. Captain Homan's suspicions of him were no doubt fully justified. But they would lead to disaster. The real brains behind this piratical undertaking would now be free to proceed. The yacht would not hesitate to fire, contrary to Homan's opinion. And Wentworth did not doubt that there must be a force of gunmen hidden somewhere aboard the ship to appear at the favorable moment to take over the *Monrovia*. If he were helpless in the brig, there would be no one to protect the women and children on board against the dreadful fate which awaited them; for a person capable of planning such a desperate piratical venture would not hesitate at destroying every living soul aboard—thus making sure that no witnesses would ever be able to testify against him in a court of admiralty.

Wentworth recognized the futility of trying to convince Homan that there must be someone else aboard who was directly responsible for the presence of that yacht. His only course now was to attempt to escape from custody, so that he would have the freedom of the ship. But with Macy standing guard over him with a drawn gun, and with the Master-at-Arms on his other side, the attempt appeared hopeless.

"Take him away," Homan said curtly.

Nita van Sloan threw him a hopeless look. He had not yet

been able to learn what Nita knew of this matter. Now he would have no further chance to talk to her.

The Master-at-Arms gripped his elbow. "Come—"

He stopped, glancing toward the dining room door.

Vinson had suddenly appeared there, flushed and wild-eyed. He did not even wait to come across the room, but so great was his excitement that he shouted out, regardless of the danger of creating a panic among the passengers: "Our radio's out of commission, sir! We can't send the message to the *Marchand*—"

And almost as if in accompaniment to his announcement, there was a low, cracking explosion off to leeward. The sound, coming over the water, was a familiar one to Wentworth, and perhaps to the ship's officers.

The explosion was followed by a low, humming sound.

Wentworth shouted: "That yacht is shelling us!"

His words were drowned by a crashing, smashing holocaust of mad destruction. The whole port side of the dining salon seemed suddenly to have caved in under a deluge of fire and thunder.

A shell from the yacht's six-inch gun had struck them squarely!

Men shouted, and women screamed as bits of the exploding projectile struck with vicious destructive force. Blood and flesh of the innocent diners were suddenly splattered over the floors, the walls, the tables. The shell had struck in the center of the dining room.

A second and a third shell smashed into the liner in quick succession. On an upper deck, Wentworth calculated. Wails of wounded and dying began to fill the air. Wentworth saw a woman dragging herself on the floor, and wailing piteously. She had been hit in the thigh. A man ran screaming, both hands clasped to his stomach, from which blood spurted.

Misery, death and chaos had struck suddenly and with merciless precision.

Wentworth felt the grip of the Master-at-Arms relax on his elbow. But First Officer Stanton Macy still held him firmly on the other side, with his drawn gun ready.

Wentworth's lips tightened into a thin line. The yacht meant business, without a shadow of doubt. These were only warning shots. They had ceased already, but they were a foretaste of what the pirates would do if the *Monrovia* continued in its attempt to escape. Surrender was the only course open to Homar under the circumstances, and Wentworth did not want to be captured by the pirates. He wanted to be free to fight them in his own way.

All this sped through his mind before the concussion of the last shell had faded from the air and he acted without hesitation. His right fist came up in a hard knot, smashing to the side of Macy's jaw. The First Officer uttered a gasp, and wilted, the revolver dropping from his nerveless hand.

Wentworth whirled, crashed a left to the temple of the Master-at-Arms, and ran across the salon.

Panic had spread among the passengers. Those who were not wounded were already trampling over the dead and maimed in a mad rush to reach the deck. They shoved, kicked and punched each other in their mad desperation.

Wentworth reached the main entrance of the salon, turned and raised his arms. His voice rose in a stentorian shout that carried above the tumult: "Everybody, quiet! The shooting has stopped. There's no more danger here. Get back along the walls, and give the doctor a chance!"

The ship's doctor, who had come running into the dining room, took one look at the welter of dead and dying, and began snapping orders.

"Clear a space, there. Get stretchers, you men. Steward, I'll need all the first-aid supplies you can muster. Has anyone here had medical experience? Good. You, sir!"

Like the efficient officer he was, he sought to take charge of the situation. But the crowd still pressed toward the exits, their panic growing.

Wentworth faced them grimly, his small pistol suddenly in his hand. "I'll kill the first man who tries to leave!" he shouted.

"Good man," said the doctor, in a whisper. "If they once get out on the decks, there'll be no holding them. The panic'll spread to the whole ship!"

The menace of Wentworth's pistol held the wild-eyed passengers back, shocked some into a measure of poise.

Nita van Sloan was already moving among the wounded, doing what she could. But First Officer Macy, getting to his knees from the floor where Wentworth's blow had sent him, spied him and pointed, shouting: "Seize that man! He's in with the pirates!"

A couple of junior officers turned, dashed toward Wentworth, and he smiled grimly. He was not to be permitted to lend his aid in this emergency.

So be it, he thought. He wheeled, and crouching low to avoid slugs from Macy's gun, which the First Officer had lifted, he raced to the door. He reached it, thrust a junior officer out of the way, and sped out into the corridor, just as Macy's gun barked behind him. He heard the impact of the bullet against the wall of the dining salon. Macy hadn't shot straight.

Wentworth saw a companionway, and raced down it. He was a fugitive on this ship now, a proscribed man, who would undoubtedly be shot on sight. And when the pirates took possession of the *Monrovia*, he would be no better off!

WENTWORTH REACHED the promenade deck and stepped out into the cold night air. Passengers were running about in wild confusion, looking up toward A Deck, just above, where the second and third shells had struck.

Stewards and seamen were hastily breaking out fire-fighting apparatus, and connecting the long lengths of hose, in the event that fire should result from the shelling. Men and women were milling about the lifeboats, while officers endeavored to reassure them.

Off to leeward, the riding lights of the pirate yacht gleamed steady and sinister. The searchlights had been shut off, but the long, white, rakish lines of the yacht stood out in ghostly silhouette against the enveloping darkness.

A blinker light was working on board her again, and Wentworth spelled out the Morse message she was sending:

Monrovia ahoy!

You have no chance. Stop your engines and break out a white flag in signal of surrender. Then stand by for our boarding party. You have five minutes' grace!

Wentworth stood poised at the rail, watching the spread of panic in spite of the swift orders of the officers. His thoughts were not of preventing panic now. They were turned to the question of how to thwart these murderous pirates. The note from the yacht had been signed "The Baron."

Somewhere, in the vague past, he had heard that name. Stories came back to him of a cashiered German naval officer who had fled to the Far East, and had recruited a crew of pirates along the China coast. That man had also called himself "The Baron." Could there be any connection?

Baron Kawashi Otuna had known that the Lee-Enfield rifle would be found in his room. That meant that Otuna knew who put it there. If he knew that, then he must also know what had become of the rifleman.

Wentworth left the rail and worked forward toward the companion ladder leading to the forecastle deck. He felt comparatively safe from pursuit, because the ship's personnel would be too preoccupied with the disasters in the dining salon and on A Deck, and with the latest message from the pirate yacht, to bother with him. And if they suspected him of being in league with the yacht, then there would be no point in hunting him if they expected to surrender.

Homan's problem was a difficult one. His first duty was the preservation of the lives of the passengers. If that could be accomplished by surrendering the gold, then he must do it. But the captain was no fool. He would understand that once the *Monrovia* was in the power of the pirates, they would destroy the liner with all on board.

"The Baron," whoever he was, would never leave a living witness to this act of piracy. The *Monrovia* would be reported missing with all on board, and "the Baron" would be free to dispose of his loot without question.

The wrecking of the wireless sending set convinced Wentworth that the yacht had active cooperation from one or more persons aboard the *Monrovia*. If he could only discover the hiding place where the body of the dead rifleman was concealed, he would have a clue to the identity of those persons, might through them exert pressure upon the pirates aboard the yacht.

Wentworth noted that the *Monrovia* continued to speed ahead, regardless of the semaphored warning from the yacht. She was zigzagging in her course, as army transports had been wont to do during the World War when a submarine was sighted.

Wentworth's eyes glowed. Good for Captain Homan! He was not going to knuckle under. Apparently he had decided to try to escape under cover of night. The man might have made a mistake in his judgment of Pierre Colain, but he had plenty of nerve!

Wentworth's mind played with the idea of Kawashi Otuna's being the head of the pirates. Everything pointed to that deduction, except for one thing—the fact that the warning message from the yacht had been signed "The Baron." Kawashi was too clever to have used that signature, knowing that it would immediately connect him, in the captain's mind, with the signature. Only one thing might reconcile his use of that name—the fact that Kawashi was so sure of success that he did not care whether he was suspected.

In that case, however, why had he bothered to frame Wentworth? If he expected to capture the ship, he would soon enough have a chance to wreak vengeance upon Wentworth for that incident of fifteen years ago in Mongolia.

Wentworth felt that he must talk to Nita, to learn what she knew. But Nita would certainly be busy in the ship's hospital, aiding the doctor. Georgia Swinnerton would no doubt volunteer also. He would be unable to reach either of them without being spotted.

But Sir John!

Sir John Swinnerton would be alone in his stateroom. Wentworth could talk to him! What Nita knew, Sir John would certainly know also!

He turned and made his way swiftly toward the companionway leading up to A Deck. In order to reach Sir John's cabin, he would have to brave detection by Homan, or Macy, or the Master-at-Arms, or any one of the officers or passengers who had seen him escape from the dining room. But he would have to risk that, hoping to pass without notice in the general confusion.

PASSENGERS WERE crowding in panic on the promenade deck, and officers of the ship were trying to herd them inside. One of the officers, using a megaphone, called out: "Everybody off the promenade! The yacht is going to fire again!"

On the white bulk of the pirate craft, the deck gun was clearly visible.

The yacht had fallen slightly behind the *Monrovia*, but it was still possible to see the figures of the men aboard her, grouped about the gun. Then came a puff of smoke, and a shell screeched, cutting the water less than fifty feet to starboard. A second shot followed the first, coming even closer. They were getting the range of the moving ship. The next try would be more successful.

Wentworth halted suddenly, staring down into the forecastle deck, where two seamen had appeared with rifles. They were kneeling by the rail, and trying to pick off the gunners on the yacht. They fired several times, quickly, but Wentworth could see that their shots were going wild. The yacht was well within rifle range, but due to the zigzagging of the *Monrovia*, close shooting was difficult

Another discharge from the bow gun of the yacht crashed into the hull of the liner, shaking the great ship on the water line. Now the yacht's gunners had the range. If they could keep it, they would be able to blast the *Monrovia* again and again.

Fire broke out below, where the shell had struck, and alarm bells, automatically connected, began to ring all over the ship. This clamor added to the confusion and the panic of the passengers. The two seamen emptied their rifles ineffectually, and reloaded with desperate haste.

Wentworth heard Captain Homan, from the bridge overhead, shouting down to the two seamen. "Who told you fellows you could shoot? My God, isn't there a marksman aboard? Get somebody who can handle a rifle!"

Wentworth's lips pursed. He could see the gun crew on the yacht, grouped closely about the gun. They were passing another shell into the breech. In a moment they would fire again. If the *Monrovia* could win five minutes' respite, she might be able to pull away from the pirate yacht. The seamen couldn't be blamed much for missing. They were handicapped not only by the rolling of the zigzagging ship, but also by the darkness that worked against effective sniping.

On board the yacht, seamen steadied a hurricane light near the gun, to enable her crew to load her. But that increased rather than decreased the percentage of error in accurate shooting by the *Monrovia's* riflemen, for the light threw elongated shadows which made it harder to judge distance.

Only an expert marksman, with a sure eye and a steady hand, could hope to make a hit. Wentworth knew he could do it. Yet Captain Homan was on the bridge, looking directly down onto the forecastle deck. He would order Wentworth's capture if he showed himself.

But Richard Wentworth had never been one to count the cost of an action. He knew what was needed, knew he could supply it. And as Homan called again, desperately, for volunteer marksmen, Wentworth raced down the forecastle deck.

Now Homan could see him, and the captain shouted: "You—Colain! Stand still, or I'll plug you!"

Looking up to the bridge, Wentworth could see that Homan

held a revolver. The Captain was leaning out over the forward rail, pointing the revolver at Wentworth.

Wentworth called up to him: "I can shoot, Captain. Let me try one of those rifles. You can always get me—I can't escape from the ship."

Homan looked down at him doubtfully. "You want to shoot at your own men on the yacht?"

"You fool!" Wentworth cried bitingly. "Can't you understand that I have nothing to do with the yacht? It is my wish to save all of us from those pirates!"

There was another booming sound from the direction of the yacht, and a shot screamed through the intervening darkness, smashed into the top of the wheel house, just behind where Captain Homan stood on the bridge. The whole structure crashed, with a thundering, crackling sound.

The master of the yacht was intent on crippling the *Monrovia*, it seemed, for the gun crew immediately moved to reload. The liner slewed dangerously to port, and suddenly began to flounder.

Captain Homan shouted: "My God, our automatic controls are gone! Mr. Macy! Take the hand wheel!"

All the automatic controls for keeping the ship on her course had been wrecked in the destruction of the wheel house. Another shot like the last one, placed as well, might cripple the hand steering wheel and throw the *Monrovia* entirely out of control, render her helpless, wallowing in the sea, while the pirates from the yacht boarded her at their leisure.

Homan made a quick decision. "All right, *Monsieur* Colain," he shouted down. "You may try the rifle. If you are telling the truth, now is your chance to prove it! Get that gun crew before they fire again!"

CHAPTER 4
A CALL FOR THE SPIDER

WENTWORTH STRODE across the deck, seized a rifle from the hands of one of the seamen. They had been shooting over the side from the forecastle deck toward the yacht, which was at an angle off their stern. It was difficult shooting at best.

Wentworth saw that Homan, as well as several of the ship's officers, were watching him from the bridge. A large group of passengers had gathered on the promenade deck, and were peering down.

He coolly hefted the rifle, then stood close to the rail, and sighted along his barrel. His eye measured the dim figures of the gun crew on the yacht. They were carrying another shell to load into her, and Wentworth's lips tightened. He could not afford to miss. In spite of the *Monrovia's* zigzagging course, they had the range, and were scoring one hit after the other. The next might disable the liner.

Wentworth sighted carefully, mentally calculating allowance for wind. He held the rifle steady, aiming at one of two men who were carrying the shell. In the dark, he could see their white faces, but little of their dark-clad bodies.

His finger caressed the trigger of the rifle, and suddenly, when he had that face in his focus, with the top of the sight just below the bridge of the man's nose, he fired!

The white face disintegrated. He had scored a hit. Twice more he fired swiftly, accurately. Two more men fell before his marksmanship.

He emptied his rifle, but made no more hits, because the rest of the crew had scattered away from the gun, taking cover. Wentworth seized the second rifle, which one of the seamen handed him, and raised it.

But he did not need to shoot. The yacht was dropping back!

A low cheer went up from the officers and crew of the *Monrovia* who had been watching him.

Homan hesitated. The exhibition of marksmanship which he had just seen was little short of miraculous. Like millions of other people, he had read in the newspapers of the uncanny skill of the Spider with firearms. What he had just seen lent color to Otuna's charge that *Monsieur* Colain was the Spider.

"I'll talk to you later," he shouted. "For the present, consider that you have the freedom of the ship. After what you've just done, by God, we have a chance to escape from those pirates!"

Wentworth bowed. "Thank you, Captain," he called back. Homan left the bridge rail, and Wentworth returned the rifle to the seaman, saying: "If the yacht comes within range again, call me."

He was more intent than ever, now, upon discovering who on board the *Monrovia* was in league with the piratical yacht. If it was Baron Kawashi Otuna, he wanted positive proof. And

49

Sir John Swinnerton was the man to furnish that proof—if it existed.

He made his way up the companion ladder once more, amid the admiring glances of the men and women passengers who had watched his amazing exhibition of marksmanship. The fire on the promenade deck was well under control, and Wentworth heard an officer say that Captain Homan was on his way down to take a look at the damage.

The damage to the wheel house, of course, was irreparable, and the *Monrovia* would be forced to limp the rest of the way across. Without means of radio communication, she would not be able to establish contact with the destroyer *Marchand*, either.

Wentworth made his way up the companion to A Deck, and found the corridors empty. All the passengers were out on the decks, watching the flight from the pirate yacht. He swung into the corridor leading toward the row of cabins occupied by himself, Nita, Otuna and Sir John. And he caught sight of the broad, uniformed back of Captain Homan.

THE CAPTAIN was walking swiftly along the corridor, evidently going in the direction of the radio room, which was situated aft of the bridge. The staterooms in this particular section of corridor were numbered from thirty to sixty, each with its own deck veranda, just like Wentworth's. The corridor was deserted, and Wentworth suddenly tautened as he saw the door of a cabin, which Homan was passing at the moment, swing open. An immaculately dressed man, in evening clothes, was silhouetted in the open doorway of the cabin for a second. In all respects this man was no different from any of the other

first cabin passengers, with one startling exception—he wore a top hat and
a black mask, which completely covered
the upper part of his face.

Captain Homan stopped short, startled, staring at the apparition.

The masked man held an automatic in his right hand, but he
did not use it. Instead, he stepped quickly back into the cabin,
and spoke several sharp, staccato words, which Wentworth
could not catch.

But those words must have been plainly heard by Captain
Homan, and must have been startling in their import; for
Homan uttered a crisp ejaculation, and reached under his
uniform tunic for a gun.

He had no chance to get at it, however, for the doorway of
the cabin was at once filled with three or four other figures.
Wentworth's eyes narrowed in incredulity at sight of them. They
were small, wiry men, dressed in peculiar, gray-green costumes,
tight-fitting like gloves, and with green helmets entirely enclos-
ing their heads.

The green men swarmed out of the cabin, virtually engulf-
ing Captain Homan. Knives gleamed in the air, flashed down
at Homan's back.

Wentworth acted with the speed of light. His small pistol
was out and barking rapidly with swift, short stabs of flame. The
green men fell away from Homan one after the other, as Wentworth's accurate shooting brought them down.

One of them swung about, raised a gun toward Wentworth,

but a slug from Wentworth's pistol caught him between the eyes and he crumpled to the floor, the gun going off aimlessly in his hand.

Not one of the green men escaped Wentworth's withering fire. But he had been too late. The green men's knives had done their work. Captain Homan lay on the floor with them, in a welter of blood, with a knife protruding from his back. The blade had been driven cunningly, so that it pierced the heart. He had died instantly.

The reverberations of the gunfire were still thundering in the narrow corridor as Wentworth raced toward the spot where Homan lay. He did not need to stop to know that Homan was dead. The masked man had known that the captain would pass this way, and had laid this trap for him. These green men had been hidden on the ship all the time. They obeyed the masked man in the evening clothes.

Wentworth meant to find that man. He leaped over the bodies of the green-clad assassins, and stormed through the doorway.

The cabin within was utterly empty.

A closet at the left contained several articles of woman's wearing apparel. A glance told him that no one was concealed in it. The bath to the right was likewise empty.

The masked man had disappeared.

Wentworth thrust additional cartridges into his pistol, and went out through the French doors, on to the deck veranda.

This was the only way by which the masked man could have fled. No doubt he had waited to see the result of the attack, and when he saw that Wentworth's gun was exacting a toll from the green killers, he had sought safety.

Wentworth leaned far over, inspecting the verandas of the two adjoining cabins. There was no sign of anyone on either of them. He inspected them both in turn, found that they contained just the usual tourist baggage. Bitterly he realized that the masked man had merely utilized an innocent passenger's cabin, along the route he knew the captain would take.

THE REASON for the attack upon Homan was obscure. There must be some definite purpose in the elimination of the captain. What that purpose was would no doubt be disclosed soon. In the meantime, all chance of capturing the masked man had gone. He had probably climbed across several of the deck verandas, entered one of the other cabins, removed his mask and hat, and casually stepped out into the corridor.

Wentworth did the same, coming back into the corridor at the spot from which he had witnessed the beginning of the attack upon Homan. Down where the dead captain lay, a crowd was gathered, attracted there by the shots.

First Officer Stanton Macy was there, taking charge. Macy was giving gruff orders to the crew, who were removing the bodies of the green men. The Master-at-Arms was stooping over the body of Captain Homan, examining the knife handle in his back.

Macy growled: "There must have been someone else here besides Homan. These green chaps weren't shot by a ghost. And it was damned good shooting, too. Look at that one—right between the eyes!"

Oscar Potts, standing behind Macy, groaned. "Good Lord," Potts sighed, "I hope this doesn't disturb my wife! She's already heard the shooting, and I've had to lie to her, and tell her that it's

A bloody, disheveled apparition
thrust in, past the guard.

our convoy, practicing gunnery. Thank God she swallowed that. The least shock may kill her. Now this thing has to happen, right down the corridor from our cabin. It's a good thing she took a sleeping powder. Maybe she'll sleep through—"

"Forget about your wife!" Macy growled. "We've got more important things on our minds. Now that I'm captain of the *Monrovia*, I'm responsible for the lives of the passengers. And I'm not going to risk them any more than I have to. I'm going to heave to, and wait for that yacht to board us, before they sink us!"

Wentworth's eyes narrowed as he listened to Macy. He had not joined the group, but had remained hidden behind an open door protruding into the corridor. The masked man had gained a point by killing Homan. Now Wentworth could see the motive. Evidently Macy had disagreed with Homan's policy of attempting to flee from the pirates.

By eliminating Homan, the masked killer had put in charge of the *Monrovia* a man who would not resist them. Macy's cold-blooded assumption of command, before Homan's body became actually cold, was an unpleasant thing to behold.

Mrs. Burgeon, who was in the group, exclaimed to the First Officer: "But Mr. Macy, why should we stop for those pirates? We're out of range, and we have a good chance of getting away. Thanks to *Monsieur* Colain's marksmanship—"

"I'll thank you to keep your opinions to yourself, Mrs. Burgeon!" Stanton Macy blazed. "I am captain of this ship now, and what I say goes. As for *Monsieur* Colain, I still think he's one of those pirates."

Wentworth's lips tightened. The worst thing that could

have happened for those on board the *Monrovia* was the death of Captain Homan. Some means would have to be found to prevent Macy from surrendering to the pirates.

Wentworth slipped away from the corridor, toward the bridge. He still wanted to interview Sir John Swinnerton, but there was something else to do first. He mounted to the bridge without opposition. Apparently the disasters which had occurred so swiftly had demoralized the discipline on board the *Monrovia*, and no one stopped him as he made his way toward the wrecked wheel house.

THE SHELL from the yacht had demolished the wheel house, but it had miraculously missed the chart room. Wentworth stepped through a pile of debris, picking his way in the darkness, toward the light which shone from the porthole of the chart room.

He walked around toward the door, found it open, and heard voices from within. He could peer in from the darkness without being seen, and he recognized Vinson and three other ship's officers. They were arguing in rather loud tones, and the tenor of their conversation caused Wentworth to stop short.

Vinson was saying: "I tell you, Sayres, I'm sure *Monsieur* Colain is the Spider. Kawashi Otuna swears he met him in Mongolia, and would recognize him anywhere!"

Sayres, a squat, competent-looking officer, sucked a pipe meditatively.

"If you're right, Vinson," Sayres replied, "then we should team up with the Spider. I tell you, the Spider's no crook. I know a chap in Midwest City whom he once helped, and I'm in position to assure you that the Spider would help anybody in trouble!"

"If we could only convince Macy of that," the third member of the group sighed, "we might get somewhere. I'd hate to see us surrender to those damned pirates."

Vinson shook his head. "In the first place, how are we going to know for sure that Colain is the Spider? If we asked him—and even if he said yes, how would we know he was speaking the truth? And in the second place, what could even the Spider do to help us? That yacht is sure to keep on our tail."

"Why should they?" Sayres inquired. "We're faster than they—"

Vinson threw him a queer look. "Don't you know why? Hasn't Macy told you?"

"Not a thing," Sayres said, puzzled.

Vinson laughed harshly. "That's funny. When I reported it to him, he said he'd tell Captain Homan, but I don't think he did—"

"Reported *what* to him?" Sayres demanded impatiently. "Come on, man, out with it!"

Vinson hesitated a moment. Wentworth was becoming keenly interested in the conversation. His mind flew ahead to possible conjectures as to what Vinson could have discovered that made him sure the yacht would be able to find them in the night, and to keep up with the faster liner.

Vinson's explanation came slowly. "First, the Chief Engineer reported that there's something radically wrong with one of the turbines. As a result, he can't get full speed out of the ship. And secondly, the radio operator reported to me, just before his set was put out of commission, that he was picking up a sort of radio beam that seemed to be coming from this ship. Do you realize what that means?"

Vinson paused a moment, then went on very slowly, as if he wanted to impress every word upon his listeners. *"It means that someone on this ship has a concealed sending set, by means of which he is sending a radio beam to guide the yacht to us!"*

There was a sudden silence among the three officers in the chart room after Vinson's statement.

At last Sayres said in a hushed voice: "Good God, there's treachery all around us. Treachery, I say! It couldn't be a passenger who is sending that radio beam—no passenger would have had the opportunity to rig up the apparatus. Some officer or seaman is doing this to us!"

He paused a moment, then went on. "That's why we need the Spider—to tell us what to do, whom to trust. If I were sure Colain was the Spider, I'd talk to the other officers, get them behind me, and force Macy to do as he's told!"

Slowly, in the darkness, Richard Wentworth backed away from the open doorway of the chart room. He knew now what he had to do. In his baggage was everything necessary to prove to these men that he was the Spider. Wentworth had thought that the Spider was dead forever. He had brought along the tools and the garments of that notorious personality merely for remembrance's sake. Now, he must use them once more.

The Spider would walk again!

CHAPTER 5
CAN THE DEAD WALK?

THE TRUTH of what Vinson had told Syres in the chart room was borne in upon Wentworth as he descended the companion ladder from the bridge to A Deck. Far off to port he could see the riding lights of a vessel. The vague shape of the pirate yacht was visible under those riding lights.

Only a short time before, the *Monrovia* had lost that yacht. Now they had somehow found the liner, in spite of the darkness and the vastness of the ocean. There was only one explanation for it—the radio beam that Vinson had spoken of.

"The Baron," whoever he was, had planned well. The presence of those green assassins on board the *Monrovia* indicated that "the Baron" had left nothing to chance. He had probably foreseen that the *Monrovia's* master would attempt to escape, and had provided the means of eliminating him, by secreting the green men aboard. How he had gotten them on, where he had hidden them, was still a mystery.

Wentworth's thoughts reverted once more to the twenty-four coffins under the care of Baron Kawashi Otuna. True, Captain Homan had said that he had inspected them and found them hermetically sealed. Nevertheless, they might, by some ingenious means, have been made to contain the green men.

He made a mental note to investigate those coffins as soon as possible. Now, he intended to have his talk with Sir John Swinnerton, and then break out the cape and hat of the Spider.

But as he reached A Deck he passed the open door of the

First Officer's cabin. A petty officer stood guard in the corridor, and Wentworth could see Macy, standing behind a desk, inside the room. Macy looked up just as Wentworth passed, and shouted:

"Wait! Colain! I want to talk to you!"

Wentworth stopped reluctantly. He did not wish to waste time with Macy now. But he could not avoid it. He turned and, passing the petty officer, entered the cabin.

Now he saw that Georgia Swinnerton was standing opposite the desk, where she had been hidden from the corridor by a tall cabinet.

Wentworth smiled at her, noting that her face was flushed, and her breasts were rising and falling swiftly, as from deep agitation. She nodded to Wentworth, but did not speak. Quickly she turned to Macy, threw him a questioning look.

Wentworth wondered what might lay between these two.

Macy said: "Leave us alone now, Georgia. I want to talk to *Monsieur* Colain."

Wentworth's eyes narrowed. It was strange that an officer of a liner should address the niece of the Advisor to the Bank of England by her first name.

Georgia Swinnerton gulped, said: "All right, Stan. Please don't do anything rash."

Macy nodded jerkily. "All right, all right. Go up to the hospital and help Doctor Murdoch and Miss van Sloan. I'll see you later." The First Officer seemed to be quite impatient to talk to Wentworth alone.

Georgia Swinnerton started for the door. "I won't go directly to the hospital," she said. "I want to stop off and look in on Mrs. Potts. Poor Mr. Potts has been so worried about his wife. He's afraid her heart will stop, as a result of all this excitement. But she won't let Dr. Murdoch or anyone else look at her. Mr. Potts says she distrusts doctors."

Macy nodded once more. "I'll see you later, Georgia."

Miss Swinnerton threw a queer glance at Wentworth, then left the room.

As soon as she was gone, Macy came around the desk, his eyes on Wentworth. "I'm afraid, *Monsieur* Colain," he said coldly, "that I'll have to countermand our late captain's order and hold you as my prisoner!"

Wentworth frowned, studying the other, noted that though his weather-beaten face did not betray any particular emotion, his lips were twitching slightly, and there was a hot gleam in his eyes.

Macy stopped within a couple of feet of Wentworth. "The way things are shaping up on board this vessel, *Monsieur* Colain, I am forced to judge that you are in league with that pirate yacht. Baron Otuna's accusation against you has been proven. I found the rifle in your cabin—the rifle with which Sir John was shot. That means that you must have helped to dispose of the body of the rifleman—"

"Not so fast, Captain Macy," Wentworth said softly. "Hasn't it occurred to you that that rifle might have been planted in my cabin?"

Macy scowled. "It might have been—but the fact that you are the Spider is against you."

"You have proof of that, too?"

"I have!" Macy exclaimed triumphantly. "You are not Pierre Colain, of Senegal. You are Richard Wentworth!"

Wentworth raised his eyebrows. "You think the dead can walk again?"

"Not the dead, Mr. Wentworth. Not the dead!" He thrust a sheet of paper under Wentworth's eyes. "Our radio sending equipment may be out of order, but we still have receiving sets in the first class cabins. Our radio operator has been taking down the news broadcasts in shorthand, to post on the bulletin board. Here's an item that just came in!"

Wentworth's eyes clouded as he read the bulletin.

New York, N.Y.

The mystery surrounding the death of Richard Wentworth, noted sportsman and criminologist, was today cleared up with a dramatic punch that rivals anything in fiction.

Some weeks ago, a body, thought to have been that of Mr. Wentworth, was found, crushed and mangled after a fall from the penthouse apartment where Mr. Wentworth had made his home. That body was exhumed at the request of the Medical Examiner, and a dentist recognized the dental work on the dead man as his own. In this way, the body has been positively identified as that of an underworld character wanted by the police. Richard Wentworth, therefore, is not dead. The mystery is now greater than ever. All New York is asking: *"Where is Richard Wentworth?"*

"So you see," Macy said slowly, "Baron Kawashi Otuna's state-

63

ment that you are Richard Wentworth was true. I also believe his charge that you are acting in concert with the pirate yacht!"

Wentworth did not bother to deny the truth of the radio news item. That it would sooner or later be discovered that he was still alive, he had always expected. All he had wanted was a period of respite, during which he and Nita might live outside the shadow of peril in which the Spider walked. That was not to be, and it was just as well, in that case, that he should resume his rightful identity.

Of course, as Richard Wentworth, he had never admitted that he was the Spider. He must not admit it now. And he must devise some means whereby he could bring the world to believe that he and the Spider were two different persons. That would come later. Now, he handed the paper back to Macy, looked him full in the eyes.

"What of this, Mr. Macy? Suppose I am Wentworth? How does that prove that I have anything to do with the yacht? You saw me shoot down the gunners aboard her, only a little while ago. Would I shoot my own men?"

Macy laughed shortly. "That shows how clever you are, Wentworth. You did that in order to pull the wool over Homan's eyes. You deliberately sacrificed a couple of men aboard your own yacht, so as to make Homan think you were innocent!"

Wentworth shrugged. There was no use arguing with a man who was so firmly convinced. "We're wasting time, Macy. Is this what you wanted to talk to me about?"

"Yes. And something else, too. Let's stop beating about the bush and get down to brass tacks. That yacht is on our tail again.

We can't hope to escape them. I have two choices—I could run, and let them sink us, in which case you and your damned pirates wouldn't get a single ounce of the gold; or I could surrender, and let them board us."

Macy paused, watching Wentworth keenly. *"Now, what would you offer me to surrender?"*

Wentworth repressed a gasp of surprise. "You mean—you'd actually betray your trust, and surrender the ship—for a price?"

"Yes. You're clever, Wentworth—damned clever. You've put me in a spot where I dare not call my soul my own. You're making me betray everything I ever held sacred in life!"

WENTWORTH STARED at the man, trying to understand what was behind this sudden outburst. Macy spoke hoarsely, with every appearance of sincerity. Something was taking place here, behind the scenes, of which Wentworth had been heretofore ignorant. If he had only been able to talk to Nita when they first came aboard, much of this might have been clear to him. Now he could only guess and flounder.

"If you'll only get a grip on yourself, Macy, and tell me just what you mean by all this—"

Suddenly, Stanton Macy seemed to lose all control of himself. "You damned devil!" he shouted. "You've made a special hell for me, and then you stand there and feign ignorance—laughing at me all the time, because you know I'll have to do your damned bidding after all. Maybe I ought to kill you anyway, and to hell with the consequences!"

A wild light sprang into Macy's eyes, and his lower lip twitched. "By God, I will! I'll rid the world of a devil! I don't care what happens to Georgia, or to me! *Now!*"

And First Officer Stanton Macy's two big hands sprang out in quick vengeful fury, twined about Richard Wentworth's throat.

Though Wentworth was a tall man, Macy was bigger and heavier; and the access of hate which was surging over him lent him even greater strength. His thick, knotted fingers tightened, cutting off the air from Wentworth's lungs. Macy's face, now red and mottled, was close to his, and the First Officer's lips were fixed into an angry snarl.

Wentworth had a choice of four different and effective thrusts to break that grip upon his throat. He had studied long and arduously in the byways of the Orient, and had acquired a mastery of the principles of *jiu-jitsu* which few white men could equal. There were four "touches" which he could employ, any one of which would render Macy unconscious, and one of which would kill him. But Wentworth wanted the First Officer to remain alive, and in full possession of his faculties. The things he had learned in the preceding few moments had convinced him that Macy should remain in charge of this ship.

He had thought that Macy might be under the order of the mysterious "Baron"—especially when he had seen Homan killed, apparently only for the purpose of putting the First Officer in command. Now that he knew that Macy was not a willing tool of "the Baron," he had no wish to harm the man. Of course, Macy might have been acting for Wentworth's benefit, but Wentworth doubted that.

He had seen too many men in the grip of overpowering emotion, not to know when he saw it. Macy had been sincere in his suspicions, and he was sincere now in his murderous attack.

Wentworth's breath was coming in gasps now. Vaguely he heard the sounds of a commotion out in the corridor, but those sounds registered with him only faintly. Macy was pushing him back toward the wall, choking, choking relentlessly.

Wentworth brought up his right fist in a smashing blow to Macy's face, but the First Officer only shook his head and kept his grip. Again and again Wentworth stabbed into the other's face, with driving lefts and rights. Macy's features became bloody and cut, but he kept his grip like a bulldog.

Wentworth was beginning to feel the effects of those powerful hands. His chest burned. Spots began to dance before his eyes. His attacker's bloodshot eyes were only a few inches from his own, and in those eyes he read the determination to throttle him to death.

Desperately, Wentworth shifted his attack to Macy's stomach. He drove his arms in piston-like jabs into the other's abdomen. Macy gasped, but held on.

Wentworth was beginning to grow groggy. He knew that his blows would weaken in a matter of seconds, that he would shortly lose consciousness, become limp, unresisting in the First Officer's vicious grip. And he knew that Macy would never let go until he was sure his victim was dead.

Wentworth's mouth was open wide in an effort to draw every possible drop of air into his tortured, burning lungs. And he put all of his fast waning strength into one last, Herculean effort. He put all his weight behind a smashing uppercut that caught Macy under the chin, and rocked the big man's head back. Macy's grip involuntarily relaxed. Had Wentworth been free to deliver that blow in a fight, he would have knocked his man out. As it was, he was weakened by those two throttling hands around his throat, by his fast failing consciousness.

But that slight relaxation on Macy's part was all he needed. He gulped in a great breath of air, and it seemed that his lungs would burst from the sudden inflow of oxygen. He followed the blow up with a driving left and right to the stomach, and Macy fell back a pace, almost doubling over with a paroxysm of pain.

The scuffle outside in the corridor had been drowned out by the fury of the fight inside the cabin. Now, however, as Wentworth's chest expanded with renewed life from the returning oxygen, the door was suddenly thrust open, and a bloody, disheveled apparition thrust in, past the guard who had been standing at the door.

The apparition was no other than Oscar Potts. He had evidently been engaged in a struggle of his own to get past the guard, and he had just managed it.

Both Wentworth and Macy stared at Potts. He was no longer the nattily dressed amateur commodore. He was shaking as with the ague. His snappy jacket was torn and ripped. His tie was awry, and his cap was gone, revealing a bloody wound in the side of his head. He had been gashed with some sharp instrument, and the blood made a gruesome pattern on his collar and coat. THE DISHEVELED guard in the corridor started in after him, staring at the panting figures of Macy and Wentworth. He stammered: "I—I'm sorry, sir, I tried to keep him out, but he wouldn't take no for an answer—"

"Never mind!" Macy growled. "Get out!"

The guard backed out, and closed the door.

Potts, Wentworth and Macy were left alone in the cabin. Potts was sobbing as does a runner who has expended the last bit of his energy in coming under the finish line. He seemed oblivious of his wounds, of his appearance, and of the appearance of Wentworth and Macy.

His voice rose in a raucous screech: "My wife! My God, she's been kidnapped! Do something! For God's sake, do something before her heart gives out on her!"

Macy stared at him, then turned and threw a glance at Wentworth. For a moment those two locked glances, regardless of the overwrought, frightened Potts. They were like two giant gladiators who were anxious to test each other's mettle. There was a measure of respect in Macy's eyes for the fighting qualities of the man he had tried to throttle. And Wentworth felt much the same about the First Officer. Any man who could take the punishment be had meted out to Macy, and still cling to his grip on a man's throat, was worthy of respect.

These thoughts were going through Wentworth's mind at the same time that he listened to Oscar Potts' rapidly rising, almost hysterical voice.

"The green men—the green men did it!" he was shouting. "They've got her somewhere on the ship. Can't you do something?"

Macy took a quick step forward, seized Potts by the arm. "Take it easy, man! Calm down. Tell me what happened!"

Potts put a hand to his head. "They came at me with knives. I picked up a chair, but they were on me before I could hit them. I got slashed on the head, and then I didn't know anything, except that they were dragging my wife out of the bed, and putting a gag in her mouth. My God, it's awful. Search the ship. They've got her somewhere!"

Potts suddenly emitted a deep sigh, and wilted. He would have fallen, except that Macy held him up.

The First Officer dragged him to a chair, plopped him into it. He stared across at Wentworth. The belligerence had gone out of his eyes. Abruptly they registered only a great worry.

He whispered, half to himself: "Georgia was going to his wife's cabin. I wonder—"

Wentworth's mind was racing swiftly. Macy was worried about Georgia Swinnerton, because she had said she was going to look in on Mrs. Potts. The First Officer was forgetting that the pirate yacht was still on their tail, that he had just accused

RICHARD WENTWORTH

Wentworth of being "the Baron," that a number of passengers had been killed and wounded by a shell, and the wheel house wrecked. He was forgetting that murder had been committed on board less than a half hour ago.

He crossed the room quickly, put his hand on Macy's arm, squeezed it hard. "Look here, Macy! You've got to trust me. I give you my word that I have nothing to do with the pirates. I admit I'm Richard Wentworth. I'm traveling on this ship incognito for reasons of my own, which have nothing to do with the bullion in the hold. I want to help you fight this thing. Will you let me?"

For a long time Macy stared into his eyes, forgetful of the slumping figure of Oscar Potts between them. Then he muttered: "God forgive me, I don't know what to do! I—I wish I could believe you. I need help!"

"Then trust me," Wentworth urged.

For a moment longer Macy struggled with himself, then capitulated. He nodded. "Get me some water out of the cooler over there," he said almost matter-of-factly. "I'll douse Potts with it."

Wentworth smiled. He turned, went toward the cooler. He had been able to read Macy like a book. The First Officer was not going to play ball with him. Macy did not want to trust him, wanted to believe that he was "the Baron." *Macy had had something in mind when he asked him to get the water!*

Wentworth walked slowly around the desk, his back to the First Officer, every nerve taut, every faculty alert. He took an empty glass from the top of the cooler, filled it with water. Although his eyes were on the water cooler, his ears were catching every slight rustle of sound and movement in the cabin.

He heard the shuffle of Macy's feet as the First Officer moved away from Potts' chair, heard the faint scrape of a gun against the leather of a shoulder holster. Macy was drawing on him!

CHAPTER 6
WENTWORTH SETS A COURSE

T HE FIRST Officer's voice came to him now, raucous with triumph.

"Stand still, Wentworth—"

That was as far as he got. Wentworth gauged his time and his distance with an accuracy which did not allow for mistakes. Macy had started talking as he drew the gun from his shoulder holster. The gun would still be in the air as he talked, coming down to draw a bead on his back. There were still perhaps two seconds, at most, before the weapon would be leveled at him.

This timing element was not a matter that Wentworth deduced by logical reasoning as he stood at the water cooler. Rather, it was a matter of sure instinct, of deep knowledge acquired from a life of constant hazard and danger. The hunter, stalking a wild elephant, does not consciously calculate how much time he has before firing, while the elephant is charging him. He *knows* when he must fire, how long he can afford to wait before pulling the trigger. Just so did Wentworth know, without conscious reasoning, when and how he must act.

And now, before Macy finished talking, Wentworth moved with the speed of a panther. He crouched, whirled, and threw the glass in a single continuity of motion that must have seemed like a blurred phantasmagoria of action to Stanton Macy.

The glass hurtled through the air, thrown with an uncanny accuracy. Water sloshed from it, but did not detract from its potency as a missile. And almost before Macy had the gun leveled, the glass struck him on the forehead, just above the right eye. There was a nasty thud. The glass did not break, for its bottom edge had hit against Macy's head. Macy's gun exploded once into the air, and he fell backward, tripped over the outstretched feet of the unconscious Potts, and fell backward without a groan.

The explosion of the First Officer's gun reverberated in the cabin, smashing against the eardrums of Richard Wentworth. Macy hit the floor and lay still, his heart coming in quick, wheezy gasps. The skin above his eye was split, and his eyes were closed. He was out.

The door was thrust open, and the guard from the corridor ran in. The man paused, staring aghast at the figure of Potts, slumped in the chair, and at the body of Macy sprawled on the floor. He raised his eyes to Wentworth, exclaimed: "You! You did it!"

His hand went for the gun strapped at his side, but Wentworth stepped in quickly, brought his fist up in a cracking blow to the man's jaw. The guard was almost lifted from his feet by the punch, and collapsed to the floor, athwart Macy's body. Wentworth had struck shrewdly and accurately. The guard was unconscious.

Wentworth jumped over the bodies and shut the corridor door, locked it. He had no desire to engage in further fights tonight—and he did not want to be disturbed for a while.

He went quickly around to the front of the desk, to rummage

among the papers. There was a chance that he would find here some clue to the strange behavior of First Officer Stanton Macy. He wanted to know why Macy and Georgia Swinnerton addressed each other by their first names; he wanted to know what sort of hold "the Baron" had over Macy to enable him to compel the First Officer to do his bidding.

And also, in the back of his mind, there was another thought—why had the green men bothered to attack Oscar Potts, and to kidnap his wife? What relation had the wife of a San Francisco businessman to the pirates engaged in this bloody business?

None of the desk drawers yielded anything of interest, and he turned away from them, baffled. He came around the desk once more, stooped beside Macy, and examined the officer's pockets.

He found what he wanted in the inside breast pocket of the tunic.

It was a note, folded carefully. It was typewritten:

My dear Macy:

Perhaps you'd like to see the same thing happen to Georgia that happened to her mother? You know what I mean. I intend to have my way, and you are going to help me. Shortly you will be in command of the ship. You know what you must do then. I need not explain further.

The Baron.

WENTWORTH'S EYES glittered with understanding. The man in the top hat and the mask, who had appeared at the cabin door when Homan was killed, must be "the Baron" himself. "The Baron" was on board the *Monrovia* then, directing the operations of the yacht, probably by wireless or radio. He was sending the radio beam to guide the yacht. If that radio sending set could be located on board the *Monrovia*, it could be used for signaling the destroyer *Marchand*.

The ship had been thoroughly searched before leaving New York, and no radio equipment had been reported found. But that did not necessarily mean that there had been none. The police and the Treasury guards were not looking for machinery; they had been looking for the dead body of a rifleman. Even if they had seen some such equipment, they might not have bothered to report it.

This meant that the ship must be searched once more.

Quickly Wentworth formulated his plans. Macy must not be allowed to resume command of the *Monrovia*. The man revolted at the thought of aiding "the Baron" to seize the ship, yet he would do it—for some mysterious reason connected with Georgia Swinnerton. And the First Officer was obsessed with the idea that Wentworth was "the Baron." He would prove obstructive, would no doubt, when he recovered consciousness, order Wentworth seized. This must not happen now.

There was only one thing to do. Wentworth must revert to his original plan of bringing the Spider back into the picture. As the Spider he could induce Vinson and Sayres to take over the ship, to deprive Macy of command.

It was at this point in his conclusions that the telephone on Macy's desk rang. A red button in the battery of lights on the

Georgia was lifted off her feet, dangled in the air.

desk glowed as the phone rang, indicating that the bridge was calling. Wentworth picked up the instrument, spoke gruffly:

"Well?"

A voice he recognized said: "Captain Macy? Sayres speaking, sir, on the bridge. The pirate yacht is closing up on us, and you directed that we stand by for orders. What'll we do, sir?"

Wentworth simulated the deep-toned voice of Stanton Macy. So clever was he at this, that anyone standing there in the room would have sworn that it was the First Officer speaking.

"Do nothing, Sayres. Wait for me. I'll be up on the bridge directly!"

He hung up, looked quickly around the cabin. He could not find what he wanted here, and he went into the bathroom adjoining. Here he opened a medicine chest, found a first-aid kit. From it he took a wide roll of adhesive tape, returned into the room and swiftly taped the hands of Macy and the guard, who were both still unconscious.

He lifted them up, one after the other, and carried them into the bathroom. There he taped their mouths, so that they would be unable to cry out when they recovered consciousness. He set the catch on the bathroom door, then stepped out and slammed it. The door was now locked from the inside.

He seated himself at the desk, and drew from an inner pocket of his tuxedo a small, flat makeup kit, covered in rich leather. He opened this, revealing several tubes of plastic material, a vial of benzine for removing makeup, and a small mirror in the cover. He set up this mirror, and then went to work with the benzine vial.

It required a good deal of painful effort, but he finally succeeded in removing the little moustache, the tufted eyebrows and the long sideburns of *Monsieur* Pierre Colain. He washed off the olive stain from his cheeks and the back of his neck, then applied vaseline from another tube to his hair, combing it with a part on the side instead of in the center, which he had worn as *Monsieur* Colain. Finally he closed the makeup kit and stood up. It was as if a wholly different personality had stepped into that room. *Monsieur* Pierre Colain of Senegal had vanished.

Once more Richard Wentworth was himself. His cleanly etched features reflected the keen intelligence that had so often brought him through the deadliest of peril. As he came around the desk, he even walked differently. He had lived the part of Pierre Colain; and it took a conscious effort for him to forget that he was no longer a French landowner, but an American.

HE MOVED quickly, efficiently. He rummaged in Macy's wardrobe, discovered an extra officer's uniform. He took off his tuxedo, donned the uniform coat. It was a little too big for him, but in the general panic aboard the *Monrovia*, no one would notice that. He could pass anywhere aboard for one of the executive officers—that is, with the passengers and the stewards. Men like Vinson and Sayres would immediately know that he was not one of them, but he meant to avoid both of those gentlemen until he was ready to meet them as the Spider.

As he finished buttoning the tunic, the telephone on the desk rang again. He glanced at Potts, who was still slumped in his chair. The man's breathing was regular enough, but the wound in his scalp continued to bleed. It was staining the whole left side of his jacket. His head hung forward now, so that the bald spot at the top of his scalp was visible.

Wentworth picked up the phone. It was Sayres again.

"Sorry to disturb you again, sir, but it's important. Vinson has been keeping his night glasses on the yacht. With our crippled engines, she can do rings around us. And it looks as if they're fixing to shell us again. There's a crew of men at the bow gun again!"

"All right," said Wentworth, still imitating Macy's voice. "Put out all lights. Clear the passengers from the decks, send them to their cabins or to the salons. Order all portholes covered. No one is to use a flashlight. The crew will have to feel their way around when on deck. And change your course by two points. If they can't see us, they won't be able to hit us. We'll be safe until morning, anyway."

"Right, sir!" There was relief in Sayres' voice. Evidently he had been expecting that Macy would order him to heave to, and surrender. This apparent change in Macy's policy was evidently very welcome to him.

Wentworth pocketed the note he had found in Macy's clothes, and stepping over to Potts, raised the man's head. Potts' eyes were closed, and his face was pale from loss of blood. But he was breathing deeply and regularly, which meant that he could not be very badly hurt.

Wentworth heaved the unconscious man onto his shoulder, pulled open the door of the stateroom, went out into the corridor. Already, many of the passengers were coming through, in response to the order he had given to clear the decks. They were going to their respective cabins, or to one of the various salons on A Deck.

They were for the most part quiet and orderly, though here and there a woman spoke in a loud voice, bordering upon hysteria.

The stewards were doing a very good job of it, soothing the women, offering to bring them tea to quiet their nerves, checking up to see that all portholes were closed, and that any lights which might show outside were extinguished.

Wentworth reflected that the crew of this vessel could be depended upon in the event of an emergency. Of course, he did not know how many of them were in the pay of "the Baron," ready to turn upon the passengers and officers at the first order from their sinister chief. That there must be some such traitors among the crew, he could not doubt, for "the Baron" could not have perfected his plans without some sort of cooperation from the ship's personnel.

The passengers were pretty well frightened, for they had glimpsed the white outlines of the pirate yacht, from the promenade deck, and they knew that the order to extinguish all lights could mean only that they were about to be shelled again.

Wentworth heard one man in the corridor say to another: "It's a wonder Homan didn't think of dousing the lights this evening, when they hit the wheel house and wrecked the dining room!"

Wentworth smiled. It was easy to have hindsight. The fact was that Homan had not believed that the yacht actually meant to go so far as to shell them. And the pirates had not merely been satisfied with a warning shot across the liner's bows, as might be expected from any humane enemy. They had at once demonstrated their ruthlessness, by landing a shell directly amidships in the dining room.

The passengers and stewards made way for Wentworth and his burden. For the most part, no one even glanced at his face. When they saw an officer carrying an unconscious man over his shoulder, they at once assumed that another victim of the shelling had been found.

THE MAIN salon on A Deck had been rigged up as an emergency hospital. Cots had been set up, and carpenters had screwed the legs of the cots to the floor to prevent their sliding when the ship rolled. There were some thirty patients in the cots, some of them very gravely injured.

Doctor Murdoch, bleary-eyed, was still working among them. Nita had donned a starched white uniform which one of the stewards had broken out of the supply box, and she was assisting the doctor. There was no sign of Georgia Swinnerton.

Wentworth carried Potts to one of the cots, laid him on it. Doctor Murdoch came over, frowning, glanced at Wentworth without actually seeing him. All the doctor saw was another ship's officer. And since there were eight hundred members of the crew on the *Monrovia*, the doctor could not be expected to know all the officers. Wentworth had counted on this when he ventured forth in Macy's uniform.

"What's this," Murdoch demanded, "another war victim?"

Wentworth smiled. "No, doctor. He's just fainted. I imagine a little gesture with smelling salts will do the trick."

He left Murdoch bending over Potts, and turned to see

Nita staring at him, wide-eyed. He went towards her, and she exclaimed: "Dick! Is it safe for you to appear as yourself? Especially with Kawashi Otuna accusing you of being "the Baron?"

Wentworth patted her shoulder. It was the first chance he had, since the day before, to be alone with this glorious creature whom he loved. This was to have been their pre-honeymoon trip. In London they were to have been married, on the threshold of a new life. And here he was, in the midst of desperate intrigue and mystery, with the hope of marriage once more gone glimmering. For now that he was known as Richard Wentworth, the Spider would once more have to be buried before he would feel safe in making Nita van Sloan his wife.

As the wife of Richard Wentworth, sportsman and traveler, she would be safe enough—provided the Spider was properly buried. But, as the wife of Richard Wentworth, suspected of being the Spider, she would be exposed to all the hatred of a bloodthirsty, vengeful underworld. What vengeance they might not wreak upon the Spider, they would seek to enforce upon the woman who was his wife.

So as Wentworth held her soft arm in his strong fingers, he knew that the happiness of marriage was not yet for him. But he did not speak this thought to Nita. Instead, he merely smiled.

"The masquerade is over, dearest. There's a news item posted on the bulletin board, announcing that the New York police have exhumed a certain dead body and have found it is not the body of Richard Wentworth. So—" he added wryly—"you see I'm alive again!"

Her face was clouded. "I'm worried, Dick—"

He cut her off. "Never mind that. I have only a minute. Talk fast, and to the point. What have you got to tell me about this situation? How did you come to change to the *Monrovia?* And how did you know that Sir John would be in danger?"

She glanced fearfully over her shoulder. "We shouldn't be seen talking together, even now, Dick. I've had an uncomfortable feeling of being watched—ever since the catastrophe in the dining room. I met Georgia Swinnerton on Fifth Avenue, and she told me that her uncle was in danger. She said he didn't know about it, but that she had learned of this danger from a source which she wouldn't disclose. She was sure an attempt was to be made upon the gold, but she wouldn't say how or when—only that her uncle would be in danger, and that she couldn't notify the police. So I acted on a hunch, and changed our sailing. I—"

She paused, as Wentworth raised a hand. Out of the corner of his eye he had seen Baron Kawashi Otuna enter the salon through the main door. Kawashi was with Mrs. Burgeon, and he was so engrossed in talking to her that he had not yet looked across the room. If he spotted Wentworth now, he would recognize him at once, might raise an alarm.

Wentworth said hastily to Nita: "I've got to get out of here. I'll find some way to see you later. Grab Otuna and hold his attention till I go out the other door!"

Nita was quick to grasp the emergency. She needed no further instruction. She left Wentworth, angled away from him, then went in the direction of Otuna and Mrs. Burgeon.

Wentworth had turned his back upon them, and was hurrying toward the side door leading into the port corridor. Over his shoulder he heard Nita's voice greeting Mrs. Burgeon.

Swiftly he left the salon and worked his way aft along the corridor. There was much to be done now, in very little time.

CHAPTER 7
TRAIL OF A TRAITOR

I T WAS doubly necessary now to interview Sir John Swinnerton. Nita knew less than Wentworth had expected, and he did not think that Georgia would talk, in view of the fact that there was something between herself and Stanton Macy.

With the pirate yacht at their heels, and morning only a few hours away, it became imperative that Wentworth have all the information possible. He must talk to Sir John, and at the earliest possible moment. But there were also other things to investigate, other measures to take.

The ship was now without an active commander. And the officers on the bridge would be expecting Macy to appear at any moment. When he didn't show up, they would go to his cabin to investigate. Wentworth must forestall that.

But he also wanted to take a look at the twenty-four coffins in the forward hatch, and at the strongroom where the bullion was being guarded by the Treasury guards.

He hesitated an instant in the corridor, then swiftly made up his mind. He took a transverse passage to the starboard side of the ship, and went forward again, watching carefully lest he encounter Kawashi Otuna. He reached the forward section of staterooms without meeting the Jap, though he did have to push through a crowd of passengers who were being herded off the deck by the stewards. Many of them stopped him to protest against the high-handed treatment, explaining that they wanted to remain outdoors to witness the maneuvers of the yacht. Some threatened to complain to the management of the line, others shouted about their constitutional rights, while still others plucked at his sleeve to ask if he really thought there was any danger. The sight of his uniform brought them swarming about him.

He avoided answering questions as much as possible, and kept explaining quickly that all passengers were being kept off the decks for their own safety.

At last he reached his own cabin, inserted the key in the door, and slipped inside. He intended to provide himself with his concealed automatics, to secure the cape and hat of the Spider, and to visit the bridge.

In the darkness of his cabin, he put out a hand to click on the light switch, and paused, frozen to rigidity in the blackness. Suddenly he knew that he was not alone in the cabin. There was not a single ray of light in the room, for the venetian blinds had already been drawn tightly shut over the window leading to the deck veranda. One of the stewards must already have been through here, in compliance with the order he had given to Sayres.

He was conscious of stealthy movement in the cabin, and knew that there was more than one person in waiting here. A foot scraped against a piece of furniture, there was a grunted order, and his eyes, grown accustomed to the darkness, discerned several shadowy figures rushing across the room at him.

Swiftly, almost without thinking, he dropped to his knees, the small pistol appearing in his hand. A knife blade flashed over his head where he had been standing, thudded dully as it embedded itself in the wall. The person who had wielded it grunted and tried to jerk it out, and Wentworth, knotting his fist around the pistol butt, drove upward in a lunging blow. His fist connected with the breastbone of a man, and there was a *whooshing*, whistling expulsion of breath. Other figures surrounded him, knife blades glittering evanescently in the dark.

Wentworth lashed out with both fists, fighting coldly, without panic. He had been in such fights many times in the past. It was evident that these attackers had been planted here for the express purpose of lying in wait for him. That they fought so silently and so savagely indicated that their mission was to kill, and not to take him prisoner. The order must have gone out to eliminate Richard Wentworth!

A KNIFE slithered past his shoulder, ripping the cloth of his tunic. Another tugged at his side. His fists pistoned in and out with the speed of striking cobras. He kept his body continuously in motion, so as not to present a steady target for those deadly knives. Again and again he felt his knuckles striking flesh and bone. He heard grunts and short oaths, the shuffling of feet as they pressed in at him.

These men, whoever they were, were not to be denied their kill. As he fought he tried to estimate their number. Four? Five? He couldn't tell. His fist smashed into the cartilage of a man's nose, and he heard a squeal of pain. A knife drove in at his face, and he swung the barrel of his pistol down at the wrist that held it, heard the cracking of bone.

There were two men in front of him now, and he could feel rather than hear the single man behind him. A knife cut at his arm, and he could feel the hot blood pour from the wound. Then there was a quick movement of feet at his back, and he side-stepped swiftly, smashing into the two men in front of him, driving them back by his own impact. He whirled, and a knife grazed the back of his left ear. The driving body of the man behind that knife *sloshed* past him, and he struck down in a chopping blow, blindly in the dark. The edge of his fist struck the hard bone of a man's head. His fist contained the butt of the pistol, and the hard ivory stock cracked the man's skull. He could hear the cracking sound, the falling body.

The two remaining attackers in front of him turned and ran. They smashed full tilt into the venetian blinds, tearing them down, and bursting out of the room onto the deck veranda. A silvery sheen of moonlight filtered into the room, and Wentworth saw that these men were dressed in the tight-fitting garments and hoods that he had seen earlier in the night in the attack on Captain Homan. More of "the Baron's" killers!

The two remaining attackers scrambled out to the deck veranda, and now, guns appeared in their hands. Evidently they had been instructed to kill in silence if possible. Now they were going to use guns!

Wentworth's eyes were cold and bleak. He stood spraddle-legged in the middle of the cabin, and waited for the split-instant that it took those men to get the guns in their hands. And then his pistol barked twice with quick staccato jabs of flame. The two green-clad men toppled backward, a hole appearing in each forehead.

There was a scuffle of movement in the cabin, and Wentworth whirled to see the shadowy figure of one of the men he had struck down, raising a gun to shoot at him. Wentworth's wrist twisted, his gun spat, and the man on the floor jerked, dropped in a limp heap. In a corner a man lay moaning, his hands over his face. It was the one with the broken nose.

And now Wentworth became conscious of something that he heard all through the short, deadly fight—something that had registered with the inner recesses of his mind, but to which he had been too busy to pay attention. That something had been a dull, booming noise, twice repeated. And now, as he looked at the man with the broken nose, he heard it once more.

He knew what it was, without looking out through the torn venetian blinds of his room. It explained why no one had come pounding at the cabin door at the sounds of the shooting. It was the dull booming of cannon. The yacht was shelling them again!

As he stepped toward the moaning man with the broken nose, there came that booming sound again, and the whole ship rocked, seemed to stagger in her stride. The yacht had scored a hit!

Wentworth wondered dully how the pirates were able to spot the liner in the darkness, with all the lights out. But he had no time for that, he could hear a confused shouting outside in the corridor, and the trampling of panicky feet. The shell must have struck somewhere in the bowels of the ship this time, for the *Monrovia's* engines seemed to be gasping, throbbing with a strange, uneven rhythm.

Wentworth stepped toward the man who lay in the corner. The fellow's green, tight-fitting suit shimmered in the moonlight. He took his hands away from his face, and Wentworth saw that his nose was broken and bloody, was spread over his face.

The man looked up, moaned, but said nothing. Wentworth spoke quickly, urgently: "Quick. Tell me who 'the Baron' is!"

The fellow did not reply. His tight-fitting helmet, sitting skin-tight on his head, made him look like some ugly, wounded, tortured satellite of Satan. A revolver rested in a holster strapped to the man's side, and the fellow deliberately drew the gun. Wentworth stepped in quickly to kick it out of his hand, covering the man with his own pistol at the same time.

"You fool!" Wentworth exclaimed. "You can't—"

He stopped, aghast. The fellow had acted so quickly that Wentworth could not reach him in time. He might have shot the man, but the green-clad killer had not raised the gun to fire at Wentworth, *but had placed the muzzle at his own temple!*

The man died without speaking a word, slumping to the floor amid the booming echoes of his own shot. He had killed himself!

Wentworth stared down at the body bitterly. He had hoped to extract information from this one, and he was balked. Evidently these green men were more in fear of "the Baron" than of death. He had failed, so he had killed himself.

Wentworth moved about in the dark room, finding his way

by the aid of the moonlight. Swiftly he opened his bags, took from them the twin automatics, and strapped on the shoulder harness under his uniform. He left the tunic open at the top, so as to have better and freer access to the guns. The cape and hat of the Spider he also took out and donned, and he slipped into his pocket the platinum cigarette lighter, in the fake bottom of which was concealed the blood-red seal of the Spider, which had more than once appeared upon the forehead of dead criminals, and which commanded the awe and fear of the underworld.

Before leaving the cabin, Wentworth carefully impressed that seal upon the foreheads of each of the dead green men. "The Baron" had chosen to make war upon the Spider. Very well, let him know that the Spider was fighting back!

WENTWORTH DID not leave by the corridor door. He wrapped the black cape around him, and strode over the bodies of the dead men on the deck veranda, clambered over the rail, and clung for an instant to the side of the great ship, far up above the swirling ocean. Then, like some giant bat, he moved along the rail, from deck veranda to deck veranda, peering into cabin after cabin. They were all dark, with the venetian blinds tightly drawn.

Behind him, far out on the sea, was the gray, grim outline of the pirate yacht. And its bow gun continued to spit fire and thunder at regular intervals. While Wentworth moved along the outside of the ship, two more shells struck, causing the whole liner to shudder. And each time the gun spoke, Wentworth felt a strange prickle up his back. The shell sped through the air toward his back, and he did not know where it was going to hit. It might conceivably strike him squarely, swallow him up in the maw of its explosion. But he clung tenaciously to his task, moving along the row of cabins. Every once in a while he would lean far back, looking up and down the black side of the liner. Somewhere along here someone must be showing a light, some signal that was aiding the yacht to spot the liner and to set the sights of her gun. It was impossible otherwise that she should be able to score such accurate hits in the dark.

At last he saw what he was looking for. Well up toward the forecastle deck a flashlight blinked on. Someone was holding it over the side so that it would not be seen from any part of the ship. It was visible only to those on the yacht and now as Wentworth turned his head, still clinging to the outside of the rail, he saw an answering flash on the pirate craft.

The flashlight up forward clicked out, then flashed on again. Its beam sprayed the side of the boat, forming a streak of light at which the gunners on board the yacht could aim.

And sure enough there was another thundering reverberation, and the *Monrovia* shuddered as the shell struck it. Wentworth, hanging over the side, could almost follow the course of the projectile. He actually saw it strike, just below the water line. The ship rocked under the impact, and he heard fire bells begin to ring somewhere on board. This last shell had done real damage.

Wentworth worked his way forward, hanging precariously by his hands. The flashlight had gone out now, but he was sure it would be flashed again when the gun on the yacht was loaded and ready to fire once more.

He was moving faster now, careless of any noise he might

make, for there was no danger of alarming the person on the deck who was wielding the flashlight. The ship had become a nightmare of sound and confusion. Any noise he could make would go unnoticed.

Wentworth wondered dully who it was that was giving the signal to the yacht. All passengers had been cleared from the decks. Therefore it must be some member of the crew.

As he drew nearer the spot where he had seen the light, he saw a white hand come over the side, clutching a flashlight. A finger moved the button on the flash, and once more the light went on.

Almost at once there was the sound of gunfire from the yacht, and another shell, screaming through the night, struck the *Monrovia* amidships.

Passengers were crying aloud now, in a panic of fright. It was evident that the yacht was intent on sinking the liner. Perhaps they relied on the construction of the ship to keep it afloat long enough to remove the gold. The purpose of the pirates was evidently to cripple her so that she would have to stop, and then to board her.

The flashlight was still on as Wentworth heaved himself up over the rail, and landed on the deck. He was only three or four feet from the person who held the flash. In the blackness his dark cloak swirled about him, making him one with the night. Only the white patch of his face showed, and his eyes shone strangely bright as he stared at the person who had turned, startled, at the swishing movement he made in vaulting the rail.

That person was Georgia Swinnerton!

Wentworth's lips tightened into a thin line. He knew that Nita had trusted Georgia; he knew that Georgia was Sir John's niece. And she was the last person on this ship whom he would have expected to find here.

Georgia was startled, frightened. The flashlight fell from her trembling hand, over the rail, thudded against the side of the ship, then dropped to the sea. She raised a hand to her mouth, cried out in a muffled voice: "The Spider!"

Wentworth stepped closer to her, peered at her in the darkness. He saw that there was agony of soul written in her features. What she was doing, she must certainly be doing in some way against her will. Some terrible, compelling force was causing her to aid those pirates to sink the *Monrovia*. Did she expect to escape the general fate when the pirates sacked the ship? Or did she hope to die with the others?

Whatever questions wavered upon his lips, they remained unasked. For Georgia Swinnerton uttered a choked cry, turned and ran!

CHAPTER 8
THE BARON'S NOOSE

WENTWORTH DASHED after her. The deck was deserted. The crew had evidently been mustered to fight the fires which were breaking out in several places, and the passengers were being kept off the decks. Sayres and Vinson were thus far doing a good job of obeying the orders Wentworth had given in the name of Stanton Macy. Shouts and protests were coming from the darkened salons where the passengers were being detained. But no one got outside. Sayres and Vinson probably guessed that someone was signaling the yacht, and they no doubt were trying desperately to locate that person.

Wentworth had found her, and the triumph was bitter in his mouth. Georgia Swinnerton was certainly no accomplice of pirates. As she raced now along the empty expanse of deck, her girlish figure appeared almost sylph-like in the dark. It was difficult to believe that she had been capable of such a dreadful thing. Yet Wentworth had seen her with his own eyes. He must catch her, question her.

He raced after her, saw her pass the two after-funnels, and come abreast of the forward funnel.

Those three smokestacks towered grim and black above the deck. Wentworth knew that the two after-stacks served the engine room, but that the forward stack was a false funnel, being in reality a ventilating shaft which sucked down fresh air into the bowels of the ship. No smoke came from this funnel. It was near this spot, at the rail, that the rifleman had stood who shot Sir John Swinnerton. And now Sir John's niece, caught in the act of aiding and abetting her uncle's enemies, was fleeing from the Spider, past the very same spot.

Wentworth was perhaps thirty feet behind her when it happened.

He was gaining on her, running swiftly and silently, wrapped in his black cloak—a mere shadow in the night, part of the darkness. So that anyone seeing Georgia running wildly would have his eye immediately attracted to her, without ever noticing the wraith that followed her.

That is perhaps why the thing happened as it did.

Georgia Swinnerton was so deeply in the grip of fright, and whatever other emotion might be ruling her, that she did not see the noose at all.

It came swirling down from overhead at the end of a long hempen rope, and it was thrown by expert hands. It settled over Georgia's head, and the knot was suddenly drawn taut.

The girl was brought up short, the impetus of her forward motion serving to tighten the noose about her white throat. She uttered a choked scream, and her hands flew to the rope, clawing desperately to loosen it.

Slowly, inexorably, the hempen line was pulled upward. Georgia was lifted off her feet, dangled in the air.

Wentworth had slid to a stop.

His eyes raced upward. He saw that the other end of the rope was being held by a green-clad man perched at the top of the smokestack. Another green-clad man, beside the first, held a gun in his hand.

Georgia Swinnerton was being drawn up to the top of the smokestack!

The unfortunate girl was already three or four feet off the deck, her hands clutching at the rope in a vain effort to relieve the strain which was choking the life out of her at the same time that it lifted her.

Wentworth threw back his cape, his eyes gleaming coldly. His two hands darted in and out from the holsters strapped under his coat, and came out with the twin automatics.

It was at that moment that the two green-clad men at the top of the smokestack saw him. The man with the gun uttered a low cry, and lifted his weapon.

WENTWORTH FIRED first at the one who held the rope. The man screamed, and toppled backward into the smokestack, just as his companion shot at Wentworth. But Wentworth had already fired a second shot, which caught the second man in the side, at about the level of the heart. The second man was thrown backward as if a gale had hit him, and disappeared after his companion, into the maw of the giant funnel.

The sound of the pistol-fire spread over the deck, echoing back out of the blackness that hung above the grim ocean.

Wentworth, grim-lipped, holstered his guns and sped toward where Georgia Swinnerton had fallen. She was weakly trying to pull the tightened noose away from her tortured throat. He bent swiftly and assisted her. She drew in deep gulps of air, keeping her mouth wide open. Wind whipped her hair in her face, covering her eyes from Wentworth.

He said to her urgently: "Don't be afraid of me, Georgia. I'm not going to hurt you. But for God's sake, tell me quickly—why did you do it?"

She hesitated, started to speak, then clamped her lips tight.

"You've got to talk!" he rapped. "What you know may help to save the lives of every person on this ship! For God's sake, hurry! Here come the ship's officers to investigate the shooting!"

From the salon aft, several figures were running down the

JOHN
SWINNERTON

GEORGIA
SWINNERTON

deck, evidently brought out by the sounds of the shots. They were approaching quickly. Georgia saw them, started to speak.

"I—I did it to save the passengers. The—'the Baron' told me he'd sink the ship with everybody on board, if he didn't get the gold. He said if I'd help him frighten the officers into surrendering, he'd only take off the gold, and not hurt anyone."

THE BARON

"So!" Wentworth's lips pursed. "And you believed him!" There were a dozen other questions that he wanted to ask her, but there was no time. The officers, accompanied by a couple of the male passengers and one or two stewards, were coming closer. They had not yet noticed Wentworth and

STANTON MACY

BARON
KAWASHI OTUNA

Georgia at the foot of the smokestack, but they would when they came closer. And there was one thing that Wentworth wanted to know more than anything else. All other questions could go by the board if he got the answer to this one.

"Who is 'the Baron?'" he demanded of her.

She stared at him a second, and her lips moved without sound. Then she whispered: "God help me, I don't know!"

Disappointment showed in Wentworth's eyes. He believed her. And there was no more time. The searching party was very close.

Silently he arose, his black cape enfolding him. He

OSCAR POTTS

gripped the loose end of the rope, which hung from the top of the smokestack. His face was covered by the low-hung brim of his hat. His hands were gloved in black. He was a shadow among shadows as he swiftly climbed the rope.

Below him, the searching party had spotted Georgia Swinnerton, and were rushing toward her. None of them so much as thought of looking up the side of the smokestack. Had they done so, they would have seen nothing but shadows against its back side and perhaps a single shadow, a little deeper than the rest, which merged with the night.

The Spider was going up to investigate that funnel. Within him there glowed the exultant spark of approaching victory. He had not learned the answer to his question—*"Who is 'the Baron?'"*—but he had learned something else. He had learned where "the Baron's" men hid. He had discovered the hiding place of the green-clad men aboard the *Monrovia*. He was sure of it now. They made their headquarters in the smokestack!

The idea was so daringly simple that Wentworth was angry at himself for not having thought of it before. It was difficult work shinnying up that rope, for the outside surface of the stack was smooth. But Wentworth made it to the top, gripped the edge.

Before pulling himself over, he glanced down at the deck. Two of the officers were lifting Georgia Swinnerton, while the others were spreading out as if in search of her attacker.

Wentworth trusted her not to tell them what had happened, or where he had gone.

He was justified in his trust, for presently he saw the small group move away toward the darkened salon. They were helping Georgia Swinnerton to walk, and she seemed in need of the support.

WENTWORTH TURNED and looked out to sea in the direction of the yacht. She was no longer visible in the dark. Without Georgia's flashlight to guide her, she had been unable to use her bow gun again. And even with the radio beam, she could not dare to come too close to the moving liner without danger of being rammed.

She could, of course, keep within a reasonable distance until morning. When day came, the *Monrovia* would be entirely at her mercy. Wentworth thought that it had been a mistake on "the Baron's" part to launch his attack in the night. He should have waited until morning. Of course, "the Baron" might have been anxious to strike before there was any possibility of the destroyer *Marchand* coming up with the liner. That no doubt explained his haste in starting the offensive before the *Monrovia* was well out to sea.

The vibration of the smokestack was intense. The throbbing engines transmitted their every thrust to the walls of the funnel. But only a trickle of smoke crowned the next stack. Apparently that funnel served the engine which had been crippled. Wentworth clung to the side and surveyed the rest of the ship.

From his perch he could see past the shattered wheel house, down to the forecastle deck, and also back toward the stern of the ship. The fire bells had ceased to ring, but now they began again. The crew was fighting a strong blaze somewhere aft, and smoke was pouring from the after-hatch. Even as he watched, flames erupted through the battens which held down the tarpaulins over the after-hatchway.

As long as the fire was kept in the hold, and away from the engine room and the oil storage tanks, the ship was comparatively safe. She could even negotiate the rest of the voyage to Plymouth. He did not know how serious the leaks were. Two shells at least had hit at or below the water line. If the pumps functioned properly, the *Monrovia* ought to keep afloat without difficulty.

But a very much more serious menace loomed with the approaching dawn. Then the pirate yacht would resume the merciless shelling.

It was apparent to him that the orders to the yacht must have come from on board the *Monrovia*. That masked man who had supervised the killing of Captain Homan was without doubt "the Baron." If Wentworth could cut off "the Baron's" contact with his yacht, prevent him from issuing further orders, he might forestall further shelling.

Wentworth raised himself over the rim of the smokestack, peered downward.

It was pitch black in there.

And that darkness had the odor of danger to his accustomed senses. It was of course logical to believe that the green men would not wait here in the smokestack to be discovered. He was sure that there were others besides the two he had shot. "The Baron" must have been careful to provide himself with a large enough crew of these cutthroats so that he could operate effectively on board the liner in the event that he needed them.

Certainly the surviving green men would not passively await discovery. They would know that the Spider would come after them. And what more natural than that they should set a trap for him?

He smiled thinly into the night. He was as sure as if he had seen it that somewhere in the depths of that funnel, death lurked for the Spider. The very atmosphere breathed it.

He did not at once climb over the rim. Instead, he clung with one hand, while he reached for his pocket flashlight with the other. The rope dangled alongside him, and he twined his legs about it, raised himself up so that he could peer into the stack without bending over. He noted that apertures in the stack fed sea air into a ventilating space between the inner and outer casing of the stack.

And then, he clicked on the light, swept its beam over the interior.

The thin ray of light gave him a swift view of several details near the top. But it was only a momentary view.

Almost simultaneously with the clicking of his light, a sharp staccato hammering began down below. Someone had cut loose with a machine gun down there!

Wentworth's ears, turned to the point of raw tautness, had caught the first yammering chatter of the quick firer, and he jerked his head back, snapped out the light.

Slugs began to march up the inside wall of the smokestack, pattering against the metal with loud, clanging rhythm. They reached the top, fanned out into the sky, then ceased abruptly.

Wentworth was clinging to the rim of the funnel with his

fingers only, allowing no part of him to show over the top. The gunner down below had done a good and careful job. He had literally wiped the inside of the stack clean with his upward rain of slugs.

The racket that the machine gun had made was deafening inside the smokestack, but it made very little impression on the deck, for the ship was noisy enough, what with the fire bells and the shouting of excited passengers and crew, and the glaring flames below decks.

Now that the machine-gun clatter was over, Wentworth noticed that the noise throughout the ship had swelled to an overpowering crescendo. Somewhere in the *Monrovia*, other things must be happening. What those things were, he could only guess.

NOW HE bent all his wits to the problem of outwitting those green men at the bottom of the stack. The things he had seen in the quick revealing beam of his flashlight had registered indelibly in his mind.

First, there was a platform some six feet below the mouth of the funnel. It was about three feet in width, and it hung by ropes that were attached by clamps to the rim of the stack. On the platform lay the dead body of one of the green men whom Wentworth had shot. The other had probably fallen all the way to the bottom.

Close to the platform was an iron-runged ladder which led down into the waist of the ship. It was for the use of the crew in cleaning the inside of the shaft.

This explained the disappearance of the rifleman whom

Monsieur Colain had shot. His fellows had no doubt dragged him across the deck to the base of the funnel, then had hoisted his body up into the stack, disposing of it somewhere below. And when the ship had been searched, the entire company of them had probably crowded up the ladder, waiting there in silence until the search was over.

Wentworth wanted to get to the bottom of the shaft without being cut to pieces by the machine gun. He moved swiftly, surely. Sliding his hands along the rim by inches, he moved around the outside of the funnel, until he was approximately at the spot where the dead body of the green man lay on the platform. Now he climbed over without the slightest sound, dragging the hanging rope after him.

He took off his cape and hat, and working fast in spite of the difficulty of handling the inanimate body, he managed to get the cloak around the dead man, tying it at the neck. Then he forced the hat down upon the lifeless head, over the tight-fitting helmet. As the man lay there, he might have been the Spider.

Now Wentworth tied the rope end under the arms of the dead man. Then he climbed back over the rim, and hung once more on the outside, with one arm over the top.

Now came the ticklish part of the operation. He tugged gently at the rope, felt the weight of the dead man rise as he pulled. Tugging gently, soundlessly, he hauled the cloaked figure up to the rim.

From down below there came no whisper of sound. That machine gunner had not been fooled. He was waiting for another hint of movement up here, to let loose with another burst. Wentworth knew that, and was careful to do nothing to set that quick firer going until he was ready for it.

He managed to get one arm of the dead man over the rim, and held it tightly, while with his other hand he loosed the rope from under the shoulders. He was now holding the dead man by the arm, and supporting his own body on the rim of the stack by clamping the funnel to him under his own right armpit. It was breathless work. If he relaxed the pressure of his own arm against the side of the shaft, he would drop to the deck below, to be crushed. If he made any noise, he would set off the machine gun prematurely.

Now, with his free left hand, he paid out the rope down *inside* the funnel, so that it was hanging alongside the iron-runged ladder. He had left the loop at the end, with its big slipknot.

Now he was ready.

He got out his flashlight, clicked it on, and held it out over the top of the stack. Almost at once he heard the chattering of the machine gun down below. He dropped the flashlight, gripped the dead man by the sleeve, and took his elbow off the rim, clinging only by the fingers of his left hand.

The slugs from the gun down below drummed a grim tattoo of death along the inside of the funnel, and Wentworth could feel the dead body jerk each time it was hit. He held it there while he counted ten, and the vicious hail of slugs continued. They were making sure that they got the Spider this time.

And the Spider smiled thinly. He let go of the dead man's arm, and the body slipped out of his grasp, fell down into the belching hail of lead. Wentworth had moved over to the left of the platform when he had hauled up the body, so that now it dropped clear of the platform, straight down to the bottom. Suddenly, the machine-gun chatter ceased.

CHAPTER 9
THE GREEN MEN COMMAND

O N T H E heels of the last echo of the machine gun, the *thump* of the dead body which Wentworth had dropped was heard at the bottom of the shaft.

There was abrupt silence. Wentworth waited, holding his breath. Everything depended now upon just how the body had fallen. He had jammed the hat on tight, but it might have fallen off. He had wrapped the voluminous cloak about the body, and had hooked it under the lining, so that it would not open—but it might have been ripped away in the swift descent of the body.

Those were things he could never know until he climbed over the top. If the green men at the bottom of the shaft were fooled by that body, they would no longer be on their guard for further sound. If, on the other hand, they discovered the ruse, they would lie in wait at the bottom of the shaft, to catch the Spider when he ventured in.

Wentworth shrugged. It had to be done. The chance had to be taken. He pulled himself up, threw a leg over the top, then swung inside the smokestack. He found the rope in his gloved hands, twined his legs around it, and slid downward swiftly, noiselessly.

He was taut, expectant of the shock of suddenly yammering machine-gun slugs. Now was the time when he would know whether his trick had succeeded or failed; and his life was in the balance. If his ruse was discovered, his riddled body would in a moment follow that of the dead man he had just dropped down the shaft.

But no sound rose from the bottom of the stack. He slid down the rope, reached the knotted noose, and stopped, hanging in air above the blackness of the pit below. He kicked around with his feet until he found a rung of the ladder, gripped it, and transferred himself from the rope to the iron ladder. Now he began the last lap of his descent. He was close to the bottom—so close that he could hear whispering voices. He had only a few feet to go to reach the bottom.

He paused, looking down. Someone had struck a light, almost directly at the base of the ladder.

The ventilating section of the shaft, between inner and outer casings, ran directly down into a large chamber, from which vents, situated in all four walls, distributed air into the bowels of the ship. A steel door led from the smokestack proper to the air chamber, and another door gave access to this room from the hold. And it was in the center of the room, directly under the shaft, that Wentworth saw the green men. There were three of them, and they were stooping over the cloaked figure of the dead man.

A little distance behind them was a fourth green-clad man, gripping a submachine gun. The three who were stooping over the twisted figure of the dead man were whispering among themselves.

The man with the machine gun called out to them: "Snap

it up, you guys. If that's the Spider, let's go. We got to join the others."

One of the three reached out and pulled the hat off the limp form. They all gasped.

"It ain't the Spider!" one of them exclaimed. "It's Kronen!"

The man with the machine gun cursed. "The Spider must be comin' down, then! Wait'll I spray him!"

He raised the submachine gun, his hand on the trip.

And Wentworth shot him between the eyes.

THE ROAR of his automatic started the others. The light was doused at once. A flashlight snapped on, and the beam stabbed upward toward the upper rungs of the ladder. Wentworth clung to the ladder with one hand, fired with the other.

The crashing detonations of the automatic mingled in hideous cacophony with the vicious bark of the green men's guns. Wentworth shot to the left, and a little below the eye of the flashlight that was staring up at him. His first shot was answered by a shriek, and the flash fell to the floor. It did not break or go out, but remained there, lighting up the feet of the two remaining green men, and spraying with brilliance the figure of the man who had held it, which lay sprawled in death beside that of the machine gunner.

The two surviving green men kept firing upward, and Wentworth, judging by the position of their feet, had no difficulty in hitting both. The barrage from below suddenly ceased. All was quiet. The acrid odor of gunpowder stung Wentworth's nostrils as he quickly descended the ladder.

He stepped over the bodies, picked up the flashlight, and

sprayed its beam around the room. His eyes lit up with interest. He noted a shortwave sending and receiving set in one corner of the room. In another corner was a pile of rifles, hand grenades and revolvers. This room was a veritable arsenal. "The Baron" had provided well for his men.

Beside the radio sending set there was an auxiliary equipment which Wentworth recognized at once as being a new type of radio beam automatic sending device. A small needle was oscillating continuously in a dial. His lips set grimly. That at least, he could remedy. He twisted the dial until the needle ceased oscillating. If the darkness lasted for a short while longer, they would lose the yacht, at any rate.

He noticed with sudden alarm that the floor seemed to be tilted at a sharp angle. The bodies of the green-clad men were sliding down toward him. That meant only one thing—the ship was listing to port. She wouldn't be able to stay afloat much longer!

Wentworth sat down before the radio sending set, and sent out call after call, watching his receiving equipment to see if it got a reply. He had no log book, and he didn't know the *Monrovia's* call letters. So all he could do was to keep broadcasting. He continued to repeat:

"Steamship *Monrovia* calling for help. Sinking with all hands aboard. Steamship *Monrovia* calling for help…."

At last he picked up a reply. His eyes glowed as he caught the message. In a moment he was in communication with the British cruiser *Recruit*. The *Recruit* was in American waters, steaming to meet the *Monrovia*, which was to be turned over to her by the *Marchand*. The *Marchand* and the *Recruit*, Wentworth learned, had been in communication, and were scouting over a radius of a hundred miles in an effort to find their charge. Wentworth was unable to give the *Recruit* the location of the *Monrovia*.

"You better get it quick," the radio operator of the British ship told him, after he had explained about the pirate yacht. "I don't think your killing of the radio beam will do any good. It'll be daylight very soon, and since you are proceeding slowly, the yacht will only have to remain where it is, to find you."

"Stand by," Wentworth replied. "I'll see if I can find any of the officers. If not, I'll go up on the bridge and take some bearings myself."

Wentworth signed off, and twirled the dial of the receiving set. He caught an anxious voice over the air: *"Monrovia!* Steamer *Monrovia!* Destroyer *Marchand,* calling the Steamer *Monrovia,* and standing by for an answer. If you hear us, for God's sake, reply!"

Excitedly, Wentworth noted the wave band, and in two minutes he was in communication with the *Marchand.* Swiftly he outlined the situation to Captain Weatherbee, whom he had once met in Washington.

"Look here," said Weatherbee, "we've been picking up a radio beam all evening that we haven't been able to fathom. I bet it's the one that this 'Baron' of yours has been sending!"

Wentworth's eyes glowed. "If I started that beam now, Weatherbee, could you follow it to the *Monrovia?"*

"You bet! And say, it'll bring the yacht there, too, and we'll bag the whole caboodle of them!"

"Here it goes," Wentworth told him. "See if your radio man can pick it up."

He set the auxiliary equipment going again, and in a moment he had his answer.

"We've got it, Wentworth!" the *Marchand's* commander exulted. "We'll be in there ahead of the *Recruit*, and won't their faces be red! They've got a couple of Scotland Yard men aboard, and we'll beat them to the kill!"

"Scotland Yard?" Wentworth asked. "How come?"

"It seems that this 'Baron' is known to them. They've known all along that he was going to try for the bullion, but they didn't say anything, because they hoped to bag him on their own side. They thought we'd give the play away by trying to grab the credit."

Wentworth said bitterly: "So all this could have been avoided if Scotland Yard had acted at once?"

"Well, maybe not. This guy that they call 'the Baron' is really a German title. He was cashiered from the German army, and he took up piracy in China. Then he went to the United States, and built up a whole new identity for himself. They didn't know who he was, but one of their agents in America got wind of this business, and trailed 'the Baron' to the dock when the *Monrovia* sailed. He was to cable what he discovered, but they never heard from him. A man was found, knifed to death on the dock, after the liner sailed, and they think it's their man."

Wentworth had entirely forgotten the little man he had found

112

on the dock. The whole picture began to take shape in his mind now. He was piecing together the little he had learned, using the information that Weatherbee was giving him as a groundwork. But as to the identity of "the Baron," he was still in the dark.

"I hope you get here in time to do good, Weatherbee," he said doubtfully. "I don't know our position. You can't tell how far you are from us, even with the radio beam. That beam will bring the yacht, and they may sink us before you get here."

"You'll have to take that chance," Weatherbee told him. "You're sinking anyway."

"All right. I'll sign off now. I'm going to see what I can do to keep us afloat."

HE SIGNED off, made sure that the radio beam was working, and went back to the wall, where the dead bodies of the green men had slid. The room was still in darkness, except for the flashlight he had picked up. He tried the switch on the wall, but it did not work. The water must have gotten to the wiring by this time. The floor was tilting at an increasing angle.

He took his cloak and hat from the dead man, put them on once more. The cloak was riddled with machine gun bullets, but he grinned as he reflected that it had had another wearer when those bullets perforated it.

He made his way out of the tilting room with difficulty, pushing his way through the hold in the darkness. Twice he passed deserted hand pumps, standing idly with no one to work them while water crept up under foot. There was not a soul about. The hold seemed entirely deserted. Had the crew left the ship?

He continued on his way through the subterranean maze of the hold.

The strongroom where the gold bullion was kept was located amidships. He detected signs of activity here and moved in behind a crated automobile, blending with the darkness.

His glance swept the floor of the hold, to spot the bodies of four or five of the Treasury guards lying lifeless, in huddled heaps. Blood spread around them, where they had been shot. The door of the strongroom was closed, but he could hear sounds of movement within.

His eyes narrowed. Whoever had killed these guards was now inside the strongroom. He tried the door. It was locked from the inside.

He waited, listening, and presently he heard the creaking of the winch. They were raising the gold bullion from the hold!

Wentworth's mouth drew down into a grim line. The crisis was coming sooner than he had expected. This indicated that the green men of "the Baron" had taken possession of the ship.

There was no use trying to break through that door. It would be easier to tackle them from the deck above.

Wentworth hastened through the hold, seeking a companion ladder by which he could ascend. The elevators would of course be out of commission if the electricity had failed.

A little further up ahead he heard the sound of human voices. At first they came to him as a faint drone, then they become louder, took form. They were groans, cries of help, shouts of agony!

Wentworth hurried. The stench of burning wood and scorched steel came to his nostrils.

The ship's list became more and more pronounced. No wonder, with no one to work the pumps!

As Wentworth progressed through the darkness of the hold with water swirling about his feet, the cries ahead became louder and louder. And suddenly, a sheet of flame burst up into the hold from somewhere up ahead. It flared for a moment, then subsided. A woman's high-pitched, agonized scream accompanied that sheet of flame. And when the flame subsided, the scream was gone, as if it had been consumed in the fire.

Wentworth went cold all over. He knew what that was. Oil! Oil would burn like that. And a woman who has been caught in a pool of burning oil would scream like that.

Wentworth raced ahead now. He knew also where the screams and the flames were coming from. The engine room.

ALL THE bulkhead doors in the hold were open, which meant that the emergency machinery in the wheel house, which controlled them, must be out of order. Ordinarily, at the first alarm of fire, the huge bulkhead doors would be automatically shut, thus confining the blaze to a single section of the vessel. If the fire gained headway now, it would spread without hindrance.

Wentworth reached the stairway leading down into the engine room. It was a spiral, iron staircase, and he peered down into the well, but could see nothing. The engine room was far below, and though it was impossible to get a view of it from where he stood, he could hear the shouts of men and women, rising in a crescendo of sheer panic.

The stream caught the man full in the chest, swept him backward like a wisp of straw.

He frowned, puzzled, for he couldn't understand how passengers had gotten down there. With the alarm gongs ringing, they should have been at their stations at the lifeboats.

He heard his name called frantically from overhead, and he looked up to see Nita van Sloan running down the steps from the deck above. She was flushed, and there was a desperate glint in her eyes.

She came down swiftly, almost fell into his arms. "Dick! I—I thought you were dead. It—it's terrible. The green men have taken control of the boat. The yacht is standing off about a half-mile away. They found us in the night, by the flames coming out of the after-hatchway!"

Wentworth gripped her arm. "Do you hear those screams from the engine room?"

"Yes, yes. That's what I was coming down for. 'The Baron's' men have herded all the first-class passengers down there. I—I think they're going to let them drown with the ship after the gold is off!"

Wentworth's lips tightened. "I'm going down. Go back, Nita dear, and try to keep out of sight. The *Marchand* is steaming toward us, on the radio beam. I've talked to Commander Weatherbee. God grant they get here in time!"

He kissed her swiftly, said wryly: "This may be the end, Nita. It was to be a glorious vacation. Well, it's turned out a little differently. Remember—I love you!"

He thrust her away, started down the spiral staircase. Nita said nothing, but followed him. He stopped, wheeled, eyeing her grimly. "I said to go back, Nita. This is work for me—"

She laughed tightly. "No, Dick. It's work for both of us. Where you go, I go. You don't think I want to go back to America—alone!"

For a fleeting second he stood there looking up at her. Then he smiled suddenly, took her hand and raised it to his lips. "I salute the bravest woman in the world!" he murmured.

Then he turned without another word, and started down.

The landing below was the platform of the boiler room. Here were three pitiful bodies, lying dead on the floor. They were members of the engine room crew. Wentworth's eyes grew bleak. He kept on down, past the boiler room platform, with Nita close beside him.

The shouts and screams grew louder. Suddenly there rolled up to their ears the staccato drumming of a machine gun. In the close confines of the ship's bowels, that gunfire sounded terrifically loud, smashing against their eardrums with devastating fury.

Nita exclaimed: "They're shooting down the passengers, Dick! They're shooting them down in cold blood!"

Wentworth hurried down the last flight of steps, came out on the platform of the engine room. The sight that met his eyes brought a low oath to his lips. The engine room was flooded. There was about five feet of water in the huge room, and the passengers, many of them in evening dress and some in their night clothes, were floundering about in the flood.

The bulkhead at the far end, separating the engine room from the oil storage compartment, had been breached, and oil was pouring into the chamber. The huge engine at the left had developed a crack—no doubt one of the yacht's shells had struck here—and burning oil was seeping out through the crack, setting fire to the oil that was pouring from the storage tank. The surface of the flood was a blazing inferno!

The fire was spreading swiftly, and the unfortunate passengers were desperately swimming away from the flames, making for the companion ladder at the far end of the room.

But one of the green men, armed with submachine gun, was crouching at the top of the ladder, and whenever the passengers got within reach of the bottom rung, he would send a burst from the quick-firer into their midst.

The heat from the flaming oil was terrible. The men and women down in that flood of fire were uttering heartbreaking screams as they realized that they were to be kept here to perish dreadfully.

Nita van Sloan exclaimed: "Dick! Those poor people—"

Wentworth's appearance on the platform, in the cloak and hat of the Spider, had been noticed by some of the struggling passengers, and they raised their voices in desperate pleas for help. The green man lifted his submachine gun, his finger on the trigger. And Wentworth's two automatics leaped from his shoulder holsters, and blasted across the room.

The green man pitched forward, the machine gun falling from his lifeless hands. He toppled off the platform into the flood below, and disappeared under the oil-covered water.

The oil-flames were spreading with rapidity now, and the passengers, uttering thankful shouts, rushed toward the ladder.

But they were not to escape so easily. Apparently there were more of the green men up above the platform upon which the first one had stood. For another burst of machine-gun fire slashed down at the miserable men and women, cutting them down mercilessly. The flames were close to them now, and if any were to be saved, they must be saved quickly.

Wentworth said to Nita: "I can't see that chap with the machine gun from here. I'll have to go down lower!"

There was a series of rungs in the wall close to the platform, and Wentworth handed Nita one of his guns, swung onto the topmost rung. He descended rapidly. Directly beneath him the flames were raging furiously. There was a row of conduit pipes near the ceiling, and it was because of these pipes that he was unable to see the machine gunner. Three rungs down, he got a view of the man. The fellow was perched upon the main control platform, from which he could command the entire engine room.

The green man was watching for Wentworth, and sighting the machine gun toward the lower rungs. He pulled the trip of his gun, and Wentworth fired at the same moment. The machine-gun slugs smashed into the wall, marking it with a line of holes that reached almost to touch Wentworth. But there they stopped. Wentworth's shot had caught the fellow in the forehead, smashing him backward with the force of a battering ram.

The way was clear for the escape of the passengers. They flocked toward the ladder, floundering in the water, moving with desperate speed to escape the licking flames that threatened to engulf them.

Wentworth reached down to help a woman who had swum to

the bottom of the rungs leading to his platform. He helped her get her feet on the lowest rung, then motioned to Nita to go up.

Back on the platform, he stood there watching for a moment. The passengers at the other end were going up in orderly fashion, sending the women and children first.

Wentworth nodded. "I guess they'll all get out in time now—provided no more of the green men come to stop them. I'm going up on deck and look the situation over. If 'the Baron's' men have control of the ship, there's no use taking these people up."

"Be careful, Dick," Nita said huskily.

He smiled. "Don't worry. Here's my other gun. You keep one, and give the other to one of the passengers. If the green men come, fight like hell! And try to get back to the ventilating room under the forward smokestack. There's a little arsenal of weapons there. Arm the passengers, and keep them ready!"

He squeezed Nita's hand, and started up.

CHAPTER 10
THE BARON SHOWS HIS FACE

T HE FLAMES in the engine room had made artificial daylight there. Now, as Wentworth emerged from the labyrinth of the hold onto the lower decks of the ship, he had to use his flashlight once more.

Deck D, occupied by the stewards and the engine room workers, was entirely deserted, with here and there a dead body lying in silent but eloquent testimony of the ruthlessness of the green men.

C Deck housed those passengers who traveled in the tourist class. There was no one here, either. But up on B Deck, hundreds of passengers had been herded back to the afterdeck, where they muddled around in wild confusion, increased by the alarming list. The decks were slanting perilously now, and flame was pouring from the after-hatch. The tourist passengers were backed up against the rails, in order to keep as far as possible from the fire. They did not seem to be under guard. The green men had evidently decided that they could perish by themselves. Some of the passengers were struggling with the lifeboats, but could not get them lowered.

Wentworth did not stop to aid them. Wrapped in his cloak, he continued on his way up to A Deck. As he reached the top of the staircase, feeling his way along in the darkness, he caught the blinking beam of a flashlight coming along the corridor. Two of the green men were forcing Stanton Macy toward the companionway leading to the bridge!

Macy's hands were free now, but the green men kept revolvers poked into his back.

Wentworth watched them approach the stair-head. He had left Macy a prisoner in his cabin. Someone must have freed him, and then he must subsequently have been captured by "the Baron's" men. They would hardly have been likely to take the tape off his hands if they had found him that way.

Macy was going unwillingly—that was easy to see. He stopped short in the corridor, less than two feet from where Wentworth crouched, a shadow in the darkness.

"Where are you taking me?" the First Officer demanded of his captors.

One of the green men laughed. "You'll see. 'The Baron' wants you on the bridge. The commander of our yacht fell down a ladder and broke his leg, and 'the Baron' wants you to navigate the yacht after we get the gold aboard."

"I won't do it!" Macy flared. "You might as well shoot me now!"

"Oh, yes, you will," his captor mocked. "Wait'll you see who 'the Baron's' got up there on the bridge!"

"You mean—Miss Swinnerton?"

"You guessed it. And you'll either navigate for us—or else!"

Macy's shoulders drooped. Slowly he resumed his march.

Wentworth tensed. He had no guns, but he did not hesitate. As the three came abreast of him, his leg muscles tautened, and he leaped up, his cloak opening wide, his arms up-flung.

A green man yelled in alarm, and the nearest to Wentworth sprang back, swinging his gun. Wentworth smashed a blow home to the man's jaw, sent him reeling into Macy. The green man on the other side of the first officer shouted: "It's the Spider!"

He tried to shoot, but Macy acted quickly, struck down his wrist. The gun exploded into the floor, and then the Spider was upon the fellow, smashing him with piston-like rights and lefts.

The man went staggering backward, out onto the promenade deck, and brought up against the railing. He raised his gun to shoot, but Stanton Macy had stopped and picked up the revolver dropped by the other green man. Macy fired six times in quick succession, emptying the gun into the body of the man at the rail. The fellow threw up his hands, and his gun dropped over the side. Then he slid down grotesquely, until he was only a lifeless heap on the deck.

Macy looked down at the empty gun stupidly, then said: "I guess I—killed him!"

Wentworth shook him hard. "Snap out of it, Macy! I want to talk to you!"

HE KEPT his hat brim low. He didn't want Macy to see his face. He had not made up as the Spider, and his features were now the features of Richard Wentworth. No one had ever seen Richard Wentworth in the garb of the Spider, and he did not mean that they should now.

"What is Georgia Swinnerton to you?" he asked.

Macy stared at him. All he could see were the burning eyes of the Spider, between cloak and turned-down hat brim. "To hell with you!" he exclaimed. "Why should I tell you anything? Show me your face!"

"I won't show you my face, Macy, but you'll tell me what I want to know. The ship is sinking. Every passenger aboard may perish. And if they do, their death will be on the hands of Georgia Swinnerton!"

Macy began to tremble in the dark. "W—what do you mean?"

Wentworth's voice was steady, cold, as he told Macy: *It was Georgia Swinnerton who signaled the yacht and gave them a mark to shoot at!*"

Macy's head drooped. "God, I believe it! I've brought her only misery!"

Wentworth put a hand on his arm. "You'd better tell me. I may be able to help."

"All right. Georgia is—my daughter!"

"Your daughter?"

"Yes. Twenty years ago, I was a master in sail, under another name. I killed a man, and was sentenced to life imprisonment. The shock—killed my wife. I escaped, changed my name, and got a job as a seaman. I've worked myself all the way up again, and the past is forgotten. Georgia was a baby then, and she was adopted by Sir John Swinnerton's sister. I've tried to keep track of her all these years, and when they came to America on the *Monrovia* last time, I told Georgia who I was. God forgive me, I should have left her alone!"

"Why are you mixed up in this attack on the ship?" Wentworth demanded.

"Because there was one other man who knew Georgia's secret—the man who is known as 'the Baron.' After I escaped, twenty years ago, I fled to China. For a while I was with 'the Baron' in the China Seas. I told him all about Georgia—and the devil remembered it. He made me agree to prepare the quarters in the ventilating shaft, for his cutthroats. If I hadn't done it, he would have told the world that Georgia's true father was an escaped murderer!"

"I see," Wentworth said softly. "And then 'the Baron' forced Georgia to signal the yacht, by threatening to expose her father!"

"That's what he must have done. Damn him, I'll choke the life out of the fiend—"

"*Tell me who he is!*" Wentworth broke in tensely.

126

"He is—"

Macy's voice was cut off by a loud explosion from the after part of the ship. The terrific detonation sent them both staggering. Sheets of flame poured upward from the stern of the *Monrovia*. There was a dreadful rending sound from somewhere as joints were ripped asunder in the framework of the great vessel.

A streaming herd of panic-driven passengers came dashing up the stairs from the lower decks.

"The engines must have burst!" Macy exclaimed with pallid lips. "It's—"

The frightened passengers swarmed about them, separating. Macy's training as a ship's officer came to the fore.

"Take it easy!" he shouted. "Everybody outside. I'll show you how to get the lifeboats off!"

Wentworth realized the uselessness of trying to talk to Macy now. He slipped out on the deck, just as Nita van Sloan appeared at the stairhead, leading a group of men, all armed with rifles, revolvers and grenades.

WENTWORTH'S EYES kindled. He had been worried about Nita down there in the hold. The explosion might have killed her. Now he wormed his way through the throng, gripped her wrist. In the press and the excitement, no one noticed the strange cloak and hat. In fact, he was part of the prevailing darkness.

Nita swung around at his touch on her wrist. "Dick! We got out in the nick of time. If we'd stayed in the hold five minutes longer, we'd be dead now!"

"Did you get all the passengers up?" he asked.

"Yes. And we found something down there, Dick. Wait!"

She led him to the staircase. The last of the passengers were up now, and he saw that two of them were carrying a limp figure.

The figure stirred, raised its head. Wentworth started. It was Baron Kawashi Otuna!

Otuna was badly wounded. His coat and waistcoat were open, revealing a vicious knife wound in the chest. Blood was gushing freely from it.

Otuna smiled wanly. "It's the last encounter, Spider," he said. "I—I didn't think to die so soon. You—you think I am 'the Baron?'"

Wentworth shook his head. "No, Otuna. I don't. 'The Baron' is a much cleverer man than you."

Otuna sighed, closed his eyes for a moment, then opened them. "Yes. A cleverer man. I, too, planned to seize the gold. Those coffins—you noticed the air-holes. I had men in them— twenty-four men. But 'the Baron's' green men knew it. They riddled the coffins with machine-gun bullets. My men perished. And—they—died—for—me, too!"

Otuna was dying. But a last remaining spark of energy made him keep on talking. "Spider! Come closer. I cannot—talk— above a—whisper. Spider, I have always hated you. But I will die without hate—if you promise me to get—'the—Baron!'"

"I'll do my best!" Wentworth said grimly.

Otuna smiled once more. "That's good enough for—me."

He slumped down in the arms of the two men who were supporting him.

Wentworth said: "Kawashi Otuna, you were an evil man—but a brave one!"

The two passengers put the dead Japanese down gently, and Wentworth swung to Nita. "I'm going forward to see what's going on at the forecastle deck. They're unloading the gold there. You take these passengers to the lifeboats. If the green men try to stop you, you have weapons now—fight them off!"

He left Nita, pushed through the crowds of passengers. They were more or less orderly now, under the direction of Stanton Macy. Two of the boats were partway down on the davits, and the green men had not yet come to interfere. They must be busy with the gold.

Wentworth went down to B Deck, from which it would be easier to come out on the forecastle deck. It was hot down here, and he could distinctly hear the crackling of the flames from down below.

Apparently the ship's crew had prepared to fight the fire here before they were driven off by the green men, for the lengths of fire hose were all laid out in the corridors. Wentworth knew that the auxiliary pump was located on C Deck, amidships, where the fire had not yet reached.

He hurried through the corridor, regretting now that he had neglected to take a gun from one of the passengers. He was unarmed. But he kept on.

HE PASSED through the tourist salon, and stopped, looking out through the broken glass windows at the scene on the forecastle deck.

The green men were raising the gold from the hold. One of

them was operating the winch, apparently upon orders from someone on the bridge, directly over the salon where Wentworth stood. Other of the green men were standing on guard with revolvers, one of them with a submachine gun.

A box of the bullion was in the air, and the winch-man was about to swing it out over the rail, to where a tender bobbed alongside the ship.

Wentworth's lips tightened grimly. He could go back and get some of the armed passengers to fight these pirates. Or he could tackle them singlehanded—without even a gun.

He chose the latter course.

His eye had lighted on a length of hose out on the forecastle deck, all ready and connected to the outlet. There was a lever above the outlet, which would start the flow of water. If the pump was still in commission, he would have a chance. If not—

He shrugged. The Spider had taken many chances in the past. What was fated to happen, would happen.

He stole silently out onto the forecastle deck, his black cloak blending with the darkness. His gloved hands reached out for the hose, gripped the nozzle. He reached up and pulled the lever. It would take perhaps half a minute for the water to come. He waited tensely. A trickle of water spewed from the nozzle. Would the pump deliver its full, powerful stream, or would it fail?

Looking up, Wentworth could see a single figure on the bridge—a masked man!

"The Baron" was directing the unloading of the gold!

Wentworth waited tautly for the stream of water. And just then he was discovered!

One of the green men, standing directly under the bullion box, spotted him.

"The Spider!" he shouted. "There's the Spider!" The man was not armed; he was waiting with a hook to swing the bullion box toward the rail.

But the man with the machine gun raised his weapon, pointing it squarely at Wentworth across the short distance of the forecastle deck, with his hand on the trip. "The Baron," leaning over the bridge, shouted: "Get him! Cut him down!" At the same time "the Baron" fired downward.

His shot missed Wentworth, but Wentworth knew very well that the machine gun would not miss. He was standing there, defenseless, with the useless hose in his hand, emitting a thin, weak trickle of water. If only that water would come!

It took only a split-second for the machine gunner to raise his weapon, and in that scintilla of time, the Spider knew the bitterness of defeat.

No use turning to run. Better to be shot this way, than in the back. He stood up straight, still gripping the hose, ready to take it.

And then, almost before the green man's hand contracted on his weapon, the powerful stream of water came!

It roared out of the nozzle of that hose like some avenging, unleashed force of nature. The nozzle was almost ripped from Wentworth's hand, but he gripped it hard, swung it toward the gunner. The stream caught the man full in the chest, swept him backward like a wisp of straw, knocking the machine gun out of his hands.

Exultantly, Wentworth swept that powerful stream of water in a wide circle, the irresistible force of it hurling the green men back over the rail like tenpins. It knocked the winch operator off his feet, took his grip from the lever. And the boom dropped with a crashing sound, sent the box of bullion down to crush the man who had been standing beneath it. The box burst, scattering yellow, precious ingots in every direction.

Up on the bridge, "the Baron," screaming with rage, was firing shot after shot down at Wentworth. But Wentworth had stepped back under the salon portico, and the slugs could not reach him.

Now he stepped out quickly, dropped the nozzle, and raced across the deck toward the machine gun which had been dropped by the green gunner.

Up on the bridge, "the Baron" steadied his hand for another shot, but at that moment a woman appeared behind him. The woman was Georgia Swinnerton. She had evidently been a captive of "the Baron," and now was her chance. She leaped upon the masked man, seized his wrist and yanked it down, just as he fired. The shot went wild, missing Wentworth by a good two feet.

"The Baron" turned, snarling, and drove a fist into Georgia Swinnerton's face, sending her crashing backward. Then he leaped toward the rail. Other green men appeared on the starboard side, and when they saw Wentworth's machine gun, they turned and leaped incontinently for the rail.

Wentworth paid no attention to any but "the Baron." He grimly raised the submachine gun, held it so that its muzzle sighted at "the Baron's" waist. His hand was on the trip, when he suddenly uttered a gasp of surprise and held his fire.

Another figure appeared on the bridge, coming up to halt "the Baron." It was the grim figure of First Officer Stanton Macy. He was unarmed, but he advanced grimly toward the masked man, and he was laughing!

He called down to Wentworth: "Leave him to me, Spider! I'm paying my debts today—all around!"

Wentworth nodded solemnly. Macy wanted to die. It was the only way for him.

"THE BARON" uttered a scream of fear, and raised his gun, fired full at the First Officer. Macy staggered, put a hand to his chest. Blood spurted, but he kept on, moving steadily toward the masked man. "The Baron" fired again and again, at close range, and every shot entered Macy's body, but the seaman trod relentlessly on. His big hands went out, seized the masked man by the throat. "The Baron" beat against the wounded man's face with the butt of his revolver.

Macy was bleeding in many places. But he did not seem to feel the blows of the gun. He only laughed again and again. He held on to "the Baron's" throat with the same tenacity with which he had attempted to choke Wentworth earlier that night.

"The Baron" struggled, screamed, struck again and again with the butt of his gun; but it availed him nothing.

Macy still laughed and choked the other. He was a terrible, bloody spectacle. And then, as if he could stand no more, the life went out of him, and he collapsed in front of "the Baron." His grip suddenly relaxed, and he slid down slowly, his mouth still twisted in grim laughter. And as a last gesture, his hand jerked up, tore the mask from "the Baron's" face.

"The Baron" stood revealed, swaying on his feet, livid of face. He turned, staggered toward the rail.

Wentworth stared up with narrowed eyes. "The Baron" was Oscar Potts!

Wentworth raised his machine gun. "Stand still, Potts!" he called.

Potts swung toward him, and the man's face was a mottled mask of livid hate.

"To hell with you!" he screamed, and stooped behind the rail. His hand came up in a moment, gripping an automatic.

Wentworth grimly pressed the trip of the machine gun. The chattering weapon sent its slugs tearing into the rail, smashing through to drive into the body of Oscar Potts. "The Baron" was literally cut in two.

In the distance, a gun boomed, and Wentworth looked out through the first graying break of the dawn to see the trim shape of a United States destroyer in the offing. It was bearing down upon the pirate yacht.

Nita van Sloan came running out onto the forecastle deck.

"Dick!" she exclaimed, her eyes shining. "You've done it! The *Marchand* is here! And Mr. Vinson and Mr. Sayres are putting the crew back to work. The green men are gone—in that tender." She pointed to the little tender, speeding toward the yacht. The yacht had started to flee, but at the first shot from the destroyer, she had hove to.

"What about the lifeboats?" Wentworth asked.

"They won't be needed, Dick. Mr. Vinson says the fire can be brought under control, and the water can be pumped out." Her eyes clouded. "And 'the Baron'—it was Oscar Potts? I saw his face for a moment, on the bridge."

Wentworth nodded. "I hope Georgia Swinnerton isn't badly hurt. Macy was her father. But it's a secret that we must keep forever."

Nita nodded solemnly. Then: "But Potts! He looked so innocent. And his wife, that he always talked about—"

Wentworth laughed. "There was no wife, Nita. He brought one of his green men up, disguised as a woman."

Nita took his hand. "It doesn't look as if the Spider can—retire. You'll have to go back to New York now, Dick, because they know you're not dead. You'll have to be Richard Wentworth again. The police will probably want you to come back and explain."

"We'll go, Nita dear," Wentworth said soberly. "But not for long. The Spider seems to be hard to get rid of—but I'll do it, Nita. He has a serious rival in you!"

For a long moment their eyes met. Then he took off his cloak and hat, and dropped them over the side. "We don't want the *Marchand's* men to find the Spider aboard," he said.

Arm in arm they went to the rail, to greet the tender from the destroyer.